THE YELLOW DOG

One of the most significant figures in twentieth-century European literature, GEORGES JOSEPH CHRISTIAN SIMENON was born on February 13, 1903, in Liège, Belgium. He began work as a reporter for a local newspaper at the age of sixteen, and at nineteen moved to Paris to embark on a career as a novelist. According to Simenon, the character Jules Maigret came to him one afternoon in a café in the small Dutch port of Delfzijl as he wrestled with writing a different sort of detective story. By noon the following day, he claimed, he had completed the first chapter of *Pietr-le-Letton* (*The Strange Case of Peter the Lett*). The pipe-smoking Commissaire Maigret would go on to feature in seventy-five novels and twenty-eight stories, with estimated international sales to date of 850 million copies. His books have been translated into more than fifty languages.

The dark realism of Simenon's fiction has lent itself naturally to film adaptation with more than five hundred hours of television drama and sixty motion pictures produced throughout the world. A dazzling array of directors have tackled Simenon on screen, including Jean Renoir, Marcel Carné, Claude Chabrol, and Bertrand Tavernier. Maigret has been portrayed on film by Jean Gabin, Charles Laughton, and Pierre Renoir, and on television by Bruno Cremer, Rupert Davies, and, most recently, Michael Gambon.

Simenon died in 1989 in Lausanne, Switzerland, where he had lived for the latter part of his life.

For Nobel Laureate André Gide, Simenon was "perhaps the greatest novelist" of twentieth-century France. His ardent admirers outside of France include T. S. Eliot, Henry Miller, and Gabriel García Márquez.

GEORGES SIMENON

THE YELLOW DOG

TRANSLATED BY
LINDA ASHER

PENGUIN BOOKS

PENGUIN BOOKS

Published by Penguin Group

Penguin Group (USA) Inc., 375 Hudson Street, New York, New York 10014, U.S.A.

Penguin Group (Canada), 90 Eglinton Avenue East, Suite 700, Toronto,
Ontario, Canada M4P 2Y3 (a division of Pearson Penguin Canada Inc.)

Pearson Books Ltd, 80 Strand, London WC2R 0RL, England

Penguin Ireland, 25 St Stephen's Green, Dublin 2, Ireland
(a division of Penguin Books Ltd)

Penguin Group (Australia), 250 Camberwell Road, Camberwell, Victoria 3124,
Australia (a division of Pearson Australia Group Pty Ltd)

Penguin Books India Pvt Ltd, 11 Community Centre,
Panchsheel Park, New Delhi – 110 017, India

Penguin Group (NZ), cnr Airborne and Rosedale Roads, Albany,
Auckland 1310, New Zealand (a division of Pearson New Zealand Ltd)

Penguin Books (South Africa) (Pty) Ltd, 24 Sturdee Avenue,
Rosebank, Johannesburg 2196, South Africa

Penguin Books Ltd, Registered Offices:
80 Strand, London WC2R 0RL, England

Le Chien jaune first published 1931
This translation first published in the USA as *Maigret and the Yellow Dog*
by Harcourt Brace Jovanovich 1987
First published in Great Britain, under the present title, with minor revisions and a
new Introduction, in Penguin Classics 2003
First published in the United States of America by Penguin Books 2006

1   3   5   7   9   10   8   6   4   2

Copyright © Georges Simenon Ltd, 1936
All rights reserved

Inside front cover author photo: © Georges Simenon Family Rights Ltd.

CIP data available
ISBN 0 14 30.3731 5

Printed in the United States of America

CONTENTS

NOBODY'S DOG

Friday, November 7. Concarneau is empty. The lighted clock in the Old Town glows above the ramparts; it is five minutes to eleven.

The tide is in, and a southwesterly gale is slamming the boats together in the harbor. The wind surges through the streets. Here and there a scrap of paper scuttles swiftly along the ground.

There is not a single light on Quai de l'Aiguillon. Everything is closed. Everyone is asleep. Only the three windows of the Admiral Hotel, on the square where it meets the quay, are still lighted.

They have no shutters, but through their murky greenish panes the figures inside are just barely visible. Huddled in his booth less than a hundred yards away, the customs guard stares enviously at the people lingering in the café.

Across from him in the harbor is a coaster that had come in for shelter that afternoon. There is no one on deck. Its blocks creak and a loose jib snaps in the wind. And there is the relentless din of the gale and the rattle of the tower clock as it prepares to toll eleven.

The hotel door opens. A man appears, still talking to

the people inside. The gale snatches at him, flaps his coat-tails, lifts off his bowler hat. He catches it in time and jams it on his head as he walks away.

Even from a distance, it is clear that he is a bit tipsy; he is unsteady on his legs and is humming a tune. The customs guard watches him, and grins when the man decides to light a cigar. A comic struggle then develops between the drunk and the wind, which tears at his coat and his hat as it pushes him along the pavement. Ten matches blow out.

The man spots a doorway up two steps, takes cover there, and leans forward. A match flickers, very briefly. The smoker staggers, grabs for the doorknob.

Was that noise part of the storm, the customs guard wonders. He can't be sure. He laughs as he sees the fellow lose his balance and reel backward at an impossible angle.

The man lands on the ground at the curb, his head in the filth of the gutter. The customs guard beats his hands against his sides to warm them and scowls at the jib, irritated by its racket.

A minute, two minutes pass. He takes another glance at the drunk, who has not moved. A dog has turned up from somewhere and is sniffing at him.

"That was when I first got the feeling there was something wrong," the customs guard said later, at the hearing.

———

The comings and goings that followed are harder to establish in strict chronological order. The customs guard approaches the fallen man, not reassured by the presence of the dog, a big snarling yellow animal. There is a street-lamp eight or ten yards away. At first he sees nothing un-usual. Then he notices a hole in the drunk's overcoat and a thick fluid flowing from the hole.

He runs to the Admiral Hotel. The café is nearly empty. Leaning on the till is a waitress. At a marble table, two men, their chairs tilted back, their legs stretched out, are finishing their cigars.

"Quick! A crime . . . I don't know . . ."

The customs guard looks down. The yellow dog has followed him in and is lying at the waitress's feet.

There is hesitation, a vague feeling of fright in the air.

"Your friend, the man who just left here . . ."

Some seconds later, the three of them are leaning over the body, still sprawled at the curb. A few steps away is the Town Hall, where the police station is. The customs guard, who needs to keep busy, dashes over, and then, breathless, runs to a doctor's doorbell.

Unable to shake off the sight, he keeps repeating, "He staggered backward like a drunk, and he went three or four steps, like this . . ."

Five men, then six, seven. Windows opening every-where. Whispering . . .

On his knees in the mud, the doctor declares: "A bullet fired point-blank into the belly. He must be operated on right away. Someone phone the hospital!"

Everyone recognizes the wounded man. It is Monsieur Mostaguen, Concarneau's biggest wine dealer, a good fel-low, without an enemy in the world.

The two uniformed policemen—one of them has come out without his cap—don't know where to begin the investigation.

Someone is talking: Monsieur Le Pommeret, whose manner and voice show him to be a leading citizen. "He and I were playing cards at the Admiral café, with Servières and Dr. Michoux. The doctor left first, half an hour ago. And then Mostaguen . . . He's afraid of his wife; he left on the stroke of eleven . . ."

A tragicomedy: everyone is listening to Monsieur Le Pommeret; they have forgotten about the wounded man. Suddenly he opens his eyes, tries to get up, and, in a voice so surprised, so gentle, so feeble that the waitress bursts into nervous laughter, he whispers, "What happened?"

But a spasm of pain racks him. His lips twist. The muscles of his face tighten as the doctor prepares his syringe for a shot.

The yellow dog circles among the many legs. Puzzled, someone asks, "You know this animal?"

"I've never seen him before."

"Probably off some boat."

In the charged atmosphere, the dog is troubling. Perhaps it is his color, a dirty yellow. He's tall and lanky, very thin, and his huge head calls to mind both a mastiff and a bulldog.

Five or six yards away, the policemen are questioning the customs guard, who is the only witness.

They look at the doorstep. It is the entrance to a large private house, whose shutters are closed. To the right of the door, a solicitor's sign announces the sale of the building at auction on November 18: *Reserve price: 80,000 francs.*

A policeman fiddles for a long while without managing to force the lock. Finally, the owner of the garage next door cracks it with a screwdriver.

The ambulance arrives. Monsieur Mostaguen is lifted onto a stretcher. The onlookers are left with nothing to do but contemplate the empty house.

It has stood empty for a year now. A heavy smell of gunpowder and tobacco hangs in the hallway. A torch beam picks out cigarette ashes and muddy tracks on the flagstone floor, indicating that someone had been waiting and watching for a good while behind the door.

A man wearing only a coat over his pajamas says to his wife, "Come on! There's nothing more to see. We'll find out the rest from the paper tomorrow. Monsieur Servières is here . . ."

Servières, a plump little man in a raincoat, had been with Monsieur Le Pommeret at the Admiral. He is an editor for the *Brest Beacon*, and, in addition, writes a humorous piece every Sunday.

He is taking notes, giving suggestions—not to say orders—to the two policemen.

The doors along the hallway are locked. The one at the rear, which opens onto the garden, is swinging open. The garden is surrounded by a wall no higher than five feet. Beyond the wall is an alley that runs into Quai de l'Aiguillon.

"The murderer went out that way!" proclaims Jean Servières.

———————

It was on the following day that Maigret established this rough account of the event. For the past month he had been assigned to Rennes to reorganize its mobile unit. There he had received an agitated phone call from the mayor of Concarneau.

And he had come to the town with Leroy, an inspector with whom he had not worked before.

The storm never let up. Heavy clouds dropped icy rain over the town. No boats left port, and there was talk of a steamer in distress out past the Glénan Islands.

Of course, Maigret installed himself at the Admiral Hotel, the best in town. It was five in the afternoon and just dark when he stepped into the café, a long, gloomy room with marble tables and sawdust scattered on the dingy floor. The room was made drearier still by the green windowpanes.

Several tables were occupied. But a quick survey was enough to tell him which was the one with the regulars, the established customers, whose conversation everyone else tried to overhear.

Someone rose from that table—a baby-faced man with round eyes, and a smile on his lips.

"Superintendent Maigret? My good friend the mayor told me you were coming . . . I've heard a lot about you.

Let me introduce myself: Jean Servières . . . Well, now—you're from Paris, I believe? So am I! I was manager of the Red Cow in Montmartre for some time; I've worked for the *Petit Parisien*, for *Excelsior*, for the *Dispatch* . . . I was a close friend of one of your chiefs—Bertrand, a fine fellow. He retired to the country last year, down in Nièvre. And I've done the same thing: I've retired, so to speak, from public life . . . I help out at the *Brest Beacon* now, to keep busy . . ." He jumped around, waving his arms.

"Come now, let me present our group—the last carefree men about town in Concarneau. This is Le Pommeret: unrepentant skirt-chaser, a man of independent means and vice-consul for Denmark."

The man who rose and offered his hand was turned out like a country gentleman: checked riding breeches, custom-made gaiters without a trace of mud, white piqué stock at his throat. He had a fine silver mustache, smoothly slicked hair, a fair complexion and florid cheeks.

"Delighted, superintendent."

Jean Servières went on: "Dr. Michoux, the son of the former deputy. A doctor on paper only, incidentally, since he's never practiced. You'll see, he'll eventually sell you some land; he owns the best building plots in Concarneau, and maybe in all of Brittany."

A cold hand. A narrow, knifelike face, with a nose bent sideways. Reddish hair already thinning, though the doctor was no more than thirty-five.

"What will you drink?"

Meanwhile, Inspector Leroy had gone off to learn what he could at the Town Hall and the police station.

The atmosphere in the café had about it something gray, or grim—impossible to say exactly what. Visible through an open door was a dining room, where waitresses in Breton dress were laying the tables for dinner.

Maigret's gaze fell on a yellow dog lying beneath the till. Raising his eyes, he saw a black skirt, a white apron, a face with no particular grace, yet so appealing that throughout the conversation that followed he hardly stopped watching it.

Whenever he turned away, moreover, the waitress, in turn, fixed her agitated gaze on him.

————

"If it weren't for the fact that it nearly killed our poor Mostaguen—the best fellow in the world, except that he's scared silly of his wife—I'd swear this was just some tasteless joke," Servières said.

Le Pommeret called in an easy tone: "Emma!"

And the waitress came forward. "Well? What will you have?" There were empty beer mugs on the table.

"Time for our aperitif," said the journalist. "That is to say, time for Pernod. Pernods for everyone, Emma. That all right, superintendent?"

Dr. Michoux was deeply absorbed in studying his cuff link.

"Who could have known that Mostaguen would step

into that doorway to light his cigar?" continued Servières's resonant voice. "No one, right? Le Pommeret and I live on the other side of town; we don't go past that vacant house. At that time of night, there'd be no one but the three of us out in the streets . . . Mostaguen isn't the type to have enemies. He's what you call a good-natured fellow—his sole ambition is to get the Légion d'Honneur someday . . ."

"Did the operation go well?"

"He'll pull through . . . A funny thing is that his wife made a scene at the hospital. She's convinced it has to do with some woman! Can you imagine? The poor man would never dare even put a hand on his secretary!"

"Give me a double," Le Pommeret told the waitress as she poured the mock absinthe. "And bring some ice, Emma."

Some customers left, since it was now dinnertime. A gust of wind blew in through the open door and set the tablecloths in the dining room flapping.

"You'll read the article I've written on this business—I think I've covered all the hypotheses. Only one makes sense: that we're dealing with a madman. We know everyone in town, and we can't for the life of us work out who might have lost his mind . . . We're here every night. Sometimes the mayor comes by to play a game with us. Or else Mostaguen. Or sometimes, for bridge, we go and fetch the clockmaker who lives a few doors away."

"And the dog?"

The journalist shrugged. "No one knows where it came from. At first we thought it belonged to the coaster that ar-

rived yesterday—the *Sainte-Marie*. But apparently not.
They do have a dog on board, but it's a Newfoundland,
and I defy anyone to say what breed this hideous hound is."

As he spoke, he picked up a pitcher of water and
poured some into Maigret's glass.

"Has the waitress been here long?" the superintendent
asked quietly.

"Oh, for years."

"She didn't go out last night?"

"She didn't budge . . . She waited for us to leave before
she went up to bed. Le Pommeret and I, we were going
over old times, memories of the good old days when we
were handsome enough to get ourselves women without
paying for them. True, Le Pommeret? . . . He's not talking!
Once you get to know him better, you'll see that when it
comes to women he could go on all night . . . You know
what we call the house he lives in, across from the fish
market? Turpitude Hall!"

"To your health, superintendent," said the man in question, not without embarrassment.

Maigret noticed just then that Dr. Michoux, who had
barely opened his mouth, was leaning forward to examine
his glass against the light. His brow was furrowed. His
face, by nature colorless, wore a look of enormous anxiety.

"Just a minute!" he exclaimed suddenly.

He put the glass to his nostrils, then dipped a finger in
and touched it to the tip of his tongue.

Servières burst into loud laughter. "He's letting the
Mostaguen business get to him!"

"What's the matter?" asked Maigret.

"I think we'd better not drink this . . . Emma, go and ask the pharmacist to come over right away. Even if he's at dinner . . ."

That threw out a chill. The room looked emptier, more dismal. Le Pommeret tugged nervously at his mustache. Even the journalist squirmed in his seat. "What's bothering you?"

The doctor was still staring gloomily at his glass. He rose and went to get the Pernod bottle from the shelf. He twisted it in the light, and Maigret made out two or three small white granules floating in the liquid.

The waitress returned, followed by the pharmacist, whose mouth was full.

"Here, Kervidon, you've got to analyze the contents of this bottle and the glasses right away."

"Today?"

"This minute!"

"What shall I test for? What do you have in mind?"

Maigret had never seen the pale shadow of fear spread so swiftly. In seconds, all the warmth had drained from people's expressions, and the rosy blotches on Le Pommeret's cheeks looked artificial.

The waitress leaned an elbow on the till and licked a pencil before setting down some figures in a black oilcloth-covered account book.

"You're crazy!" Servières exclaimed with some effort.

It rang false. The pharmacist held the bottle in one hand, a glass in the other.

"Strychnine," whispered the doctor.

He shoved the pharmacist out the door and came back to the table, his head low, his complexion looking yellowish.

"What makes you think—" Maigret began.

"I don't know—just a fluke . . . I saw a grain of white powder in my glass, and the smell seemed odd to me."

"The power of suggestion!" declared the journalist. "If I told that one in my article tomorrow, it would close every bistro in Finistère."

"You always drink Pernod?"

"Every evening before dinner. Emma's so used to it that she brings the bottle as soon as she sees our beer mugs are empty. We have our little habits. Evenings, it's calvados."

Maigret went over to the liqueur shelf, reached for a bottle of calvados.

"Not that one. The flask with the broad bottom."

He picked it up, turned it in the light, saw a few specks of white powder. But he said nothing. It was unnecessary. The others had understood.

Inspector Leroy entered and announced offhandedly, "Well, the police haven't seen anything suspicious—no drifters reported in the vicinity. They don't understand it."

The silence in the room suddenly registered, the dense throat-grabbing anguish. Tobacco smoke coiled around the electric lights. The green felt of the billiard table spread like a trimmed lawn. There were a few cigar butts on the floor in the sawdust, along with gobs of spittle.

"Seven, carry one . . ." Emma counted, wetting the tip of her pencil. Then, raising her head, she called into the wings, "Coming, madame!"

Maigret tamped his pipe. Dr. Michoux stared stubbornly at the floor, and his nose looked more crooked than ever. Le Pommeret's shoes gleamed as if they had never been used for walking. Servières shrugged his shoulders from time to time as he mumbled to himself.

All eyes turned toward the pharmacist when he came back with the bottle and the empty glass.

He had run, and was breathless. At the door, he kicked backward, to drive something away, muttering "Filthy mutt!"

He was no sooner inside the café than he asked: "It's a joke, isn't it? Nobody drank any?"

"Well?"

"It's strychnine, yes! Someone must have put it into the bottle less than half an hour ago." He looked with horror at the full glasses, at the five silent men.

"What's all this about? It's outrageous! I have every right to know! Last night, a man was shot right near my house, and today . . ."

Maigret took the bottle from his hand. Emma came back from the dining room, impassive, and from over the till turned toward them her long face with its sunken eyes and thin lips. Her Breton lace cap was slipping as usual to the left on her unkempt hair, which it did no matter how often she pushed it back in place.

Le Pommeret strode back and forth, his eyes on the gleam of his shoes. Servières, unmoving, stared at the glasses, then suddenly, his voice choked by a sob of terror, cried, "Good God!"

The doctor hunched his shoulders.

2

THE DOCTOR IN SLIPPERS

Inspector Leroy, who was twenty-five years old, looked more like what's called a well-bred young man than a police inspector.

He had just got out of college. This was his first case, and for the past few minutes he had been watching Maigret unhappily, trying to catch his attention. Finally, blushing, he whispered, "Excuse me, superintendent . . . but . . . the fingerprints."

He must have thought that his chief belonged to the old school and was unaware of the value of scientific procedures, because Maigret merely puffed on his pipe and said, "If you want . . ."

That was the last seen of Inspector Leroy, who carefully carried the bottle and glasses off to his room and spent the evening constructing a model package—he carried the instructions in his pocket—specifically developed for transporting objects without losing the fingerprints on them.

Maigret took a seat in the corner of the café. The proprietor, in white smock and chef's toque, looked round his establishment as if it had been devastated by a cyclone.

The pharmacist had talked. People could be heard whispering outside.

Jean Servières was the first to put his hat on. "Well, enough of this. I'm married, and Madame Servières is expecting me. I'll see you later, superintendent."

Le Pommeret stopped his pacing. "Wait for me. I'm going home to dinner too . . . You staying, Michoux?"

The doctor only shrugged.

The pharmacist was determined to play an important part. Maigret heard him tell the proprietor: ". . . and of course it's imperative to analyze the contents of all the bottles! . . . There's someone here from the police; all he has to do is give me the order."

There were over sixty bottles of various aperitifs and liqueurs on the shelves.

"What do you think, superintendent?"

"It's an idea . . . Well, yes, that might be wise."

The pharmacist was short, thin, and nervous. He fussed three times as much as necessary. Someone had to get him a bottle crate. Then he phoned a café in the Old Town to tell his assistant he needed him.

Bareheaded, he shuttled between the Admiral and his shop five or six times, but found the time to toss a word here and there to the spectators gathered on the pavement.

"What's to become of me if they carry off all my liquor?" whimpered the proprietor. "And no one's even thinking about eating! You're not having dinner, superintendent? . . . And you, doctor? Are you going home?"

"No. My mother's gone to Paris, and the maid's off."

"You're sleeping here, then?"

———

It was raining. The streets were running with black mud. The wind was rattling the blinds on the second floor. Maigret had eaten in the dining room, not far from the table where the doctor sat, looking despondent.

Beyond the little green windowpanes, inquisitive faces moved, sometimes pressing up to the glass. The waitress was gone for half an hour, long enough to have her own dinner. Then she took up her customary place, to the right of the till, one elbow resting on it, a towel in her hand.

"Give me a bottle of beer," Maigret said.

He was well aware that the doctor was watching him as he drank, and then afterward, as if waiting for signs of poisoning.

Jean Servières did not return, as he had said he would. Nor did Le Pommeret. Apparently no one cared to enter the café, still less to have a drink. Word had spread that all the bottles were poisoned. "Enough to kill off the whole town!"

From his house out near White Sands beach, the mayor telephoned to find out what was happening. After that, all was gloomy silence. In a corner, Michoux leafed through newspapers without reading them. The waitress did not move. Maigret smoked placidly, and from time to time the proprietor looked in, as though to make sure there had been no new calamity.

The clock in the Old Town sounded the hours and the half hours. On the pavement, the shuffling footsteps and talking died away. Then there was nothing but the monotonous moan of the wind and the sound of the rain beating on the windows.

"You're spending the night here?" Maigret asked the doctor.

In the silence, the mere act of speaking aloud was disquieting.

"Yes . . . I do that sometimes . . . I live with my mother, about a mile outside town—in a huge house . . . My mother's gone to Paris for a few days, as I said, and the maid asked for time off to go to her brother's wedding."

He rose, hesitated, then said abruptly, "Good night." And he disappeared up the stairs. He could soon be heard taking off his shoes, just over Maigret's head. No one was left in the café but the waitress and the superintendent.

"Come here!" he said to her, leaning back in his chair. And as she stood stiffly before him he added, "Sit down . . . How old are you?"

"Twenty-four."

There was an exaggerated humility about her. Her cowed eyes, her way of gliding noiselessly and carefully about, of quaking with anxiety at the slightest word, were the very image of a scullery maid accustomed to hardship. And yet he sensed, beneath that image, glints of pride held firmly in check.

She was anemic. Her flat chest was not formed to rouse

desire. Nevertheless, she had an odd attraction, perhaps because she seemed troubled, discouraged, unhealthy.

"What did you do before you came to work here?"

"I'm an orphan. My father and brother were lost at sea, on the ketch *Three Kings*. My mother'd died long before . . . I used to be a salesgirl at the stationery shop near the post office . . ."

What was she watching for, with her restless glance?

"You have a lover?"

She turned away without answering. Maigret watched her face steadily, puffed on his pipe slowly, and took a swallow of beer. "There must be customers who make a play for you! . . . Those men who were here earlier— they're regulars, they come every evening, and they like good-looking girls . . . . Come! Which one?"

Her pale face twisted wearily as she said, "The doctor, mainly . . ."

"You're his mistress?"

She looked at him with a faint impulse of trust.

"He has others too . . . Sometimes me, when he feels like it. He'll stay here for the night, and tell me to come to his room."

Maigret had rarely heard a confession so flat in tone.

"Does he give you anything?"

"Yes . . . not always. Two or three times, on my day off, he's had me go to his house. Like the day before yesterday . . . while his mother's away . . . But he has other girls."

"And Monsieur Le Pommeret?"

"The same thing—except I only went to his house once, a long time ago. A woman from the sardine-packing plant was there, and . . . I didn't want that! They get new girls every week."

"Monsieur Servières too?"

"Not the same. He's married. They say he goes into Brest to play around. Here, he doesn't do more than joke a little, or he'll give me a pinch."

It was still raining. From the distance came the sound of a foghorn, probably from a ship trying to find its way into port.

"And that's the way it goes all year round?"

"Not all year . . . In the winter, they're all alone here. They'll drink once in a while with some traveling sales-man . . . But in the summer there are people around. The hotel is full. At night, ten or fifteen of them get together to drink champagne or throw a party at somebody's house. There are lots of cars, pretty women . . . And we're really busy here . . . In summer, I don't do the serving—there are waiters. I'm downstairs then, washing dishes."

What could she be looking around for? She was fidget-ing on the edge of her chair and seemed ready to snap to attention.

A shrill bell sounded. She looked at Maigret, then at the electric panel behind the till. "Will you excuse me?"

She went upstairs. The superintendent heard footsteps, an indistinct murmur of voices in the doctor's room.

The pharmacist came in, a little drunk.

"All done, superintendent! Forty-eight bottles analyzed, and carefully. I promise you that! Not a trace of poison except in the Pernod and the calvados. The proprietor can take back all his stock . . . So, now, what do you think, just between you and me? Anarchists—right?"

Emma returned, stepped outside to close the shutters, and then waited by the door to lock up.

"Well?" said Maigret, when they were alone again.

She turned her head away without answering, unexpectedly embarrassed, and the superintendent felt that if he pressed her, even a little, she would burst into tears.

"Good night, child!" he said.

———

When Maigret went downstairs the next morning, the sky was so dark with clouds, he thought he must be the first one up. From his window, he had seen a solitary crane at work, unloading a sand barge in the deserted port, and, in the streets, a few umbrellas and raincoats hurrying along close to the buildings.

Halfway down the stairs, he had passed a traveling salesman, who had just arrived; a porter was carrying his bags up.

Emma was sweeping the café. On a marble table stood a cup with some coffee stagnating in the bottom.

"Was that my inspector's?" Maigret asked.

"A while ago he asked the way to the station. He was carrying a big package."

"And the doctor?"

"I took him his breakfast upstairs. He's sick. He doesn't want to go out."

And the broom went on stirring the mixture of debris and sawdust. "What will you have?"

"Black coffee."

She had to pass close to him to reach the kitchen. When she did, he gripped her shoulders with his heavy paws and looked her in the eyes. His manner both gruff and kindly, he said: "Tell me, Emma . . ."

She tried only a timid move to get free, then stood motionless, trembling and making herself as small as possible.

"Just between us, now, what do you know about all this? . . . Quiet! You're about to lie! You're a sad little girl, and I don't mean to make trouble for you . . . Look at me! The bottle, eh? Tell me, now . . ."

"I swear—"

"Don't bother swearing."

"It wasn't me!"

"For heaven's sake, I know it wasn't you! But who was it?"

Her eyelids swelled suddenly. Tears poured out. Her lower lip throbbed. The waitress looked so touching that Maigret loosened his grip. "The doctor . . . last night?"

"No! . . . It wasn't for what you think."

"What did he want?"

"He asked me the same thing you did. He threatened me. He wanted me to tell him who'd been handling the bottles. He nearly hit me . . . And I don't know! On my mother's head, I swear—"

"Bring me my coffee."

It was eight o'clock. Maigret went out to buy some tobacco and took a walk around the town. When he came back, about ten, the doctor was downstairs in the café, in his slippers and with a foulard around his neck in place of a collar. His features were drawn, his red hair tousled.

"You're not looking in very good shape."

"I'm sick . . . I should have expected it. Kidney trouble. The slightest upset or excitement, and it shows up. I didn't get a wink of sleep last night." He kept watching the door.

"You're not going back to your house?"

"No one's there. I'm in better hands here."

He had sent out for all the morning papers, and they lay on his table. "You haven't seen my friends? Servières? Le Pommeret? . . . It's odd they haven't turned up to see if anything's happened."

"Oh, they're probably still asleep," Maigret mumbled. "Incidentally, I haven't seen that awful yellow dog . . . Emma, have you seen any more of that dog? . . . No? Here comes Leroy. He may have run across him in the street . . . What's new, Leroy?"

"The bottles and the glasses are on their way to the laboratory. I stopped by the police station and the Town Hall . . . You were asking about the dog, I think? Apparently some peasant saw him this morning in Dr. Michoux's garden."

"In *my* garden?" The doctor jumped. His pale hands shook. "What was he doing in *my* garden?"

"From what I was told, he was lying on the doorstep. When the peasant approached, he growled so viciously that the man decided to give him a wide berth."

Maigret was watching their faces from the corner of his eye. "Now, doctor, why don't we take a walk over to your house together?"

A strained smile. "In this rain? In my condition? That would put me in bed for a week . . . What does that dog matter? Just an ordinary stray, probably."

Maigret put on his hat and coat.

"Where are you going?"

"I don't know. Get a breath of air. You coming with me, Leroy?"

When they were outside, they could still see the doctor's long head, distorted by the windowpanes, which made it even longer and gave it a greenish tinge.

"Where are we going?" asked the young man.

Maigret shrugged his shoulders. He wandered for a quarter of an hour around the harbor, as if he were interested in boats. At the jetty, he turned right, onto a road whose signpost indicated it was the way to White Sands.

Leroy cleared his throat. "I wish we'd had a chance to analyze the cigarette ashes they found in the hallway of the empty house—"

"What do you think of Emma?" Maigret interrupted.

"I . . . I think . . . The problem, as I see it—especially in a place like this, where everyone knows everyone else—the problem must have been getting hold of such an amount of strychnine."

"That's not what I'm asking you . . . Would you, for instance, be interested in making love to her?"

The poor inspector could find nothing to say.

Maigret made him stop and open his coat so that he could light his pipe away from the wind.

———

The beach at White Sands, rimmed by a few houses—one, grand enough to rate the term "château," belonged to the mayor—stretches between two rocky headlands, about a mile from the center of town.

Maigret and his companion waded through the sand and the seaweed, scarcely looking at the empty, shuttered houses.

Beyond the beach, the land rises. Steep rocks crowned with firs plunge into the sea.

A large sign read: *White Sands Property Company.* A map indicated with one color the plots already sold, and with another those still available. A wooden booth was labeled *Sales Office.* Beneath were the words: *Address inquiries to Monsieur Ernest Michoux, Director.*

In the summertime, the whole place was probably bright and cheerful, freshly painted. But in the rain and the mud, with the din of the surf, it was sinister.

In the center of the cleared area stood a big new house of gray stone, with a terrace, an ornamental pool, and flower beds laid out but not yet planted.

Farther along were the foundations of other houses, and stretches of wall that already indicated the layout.

Some windowpanes were missing in the booth. Piles of sand stood waiting to be spread on the new road, which was half blocked now by a steamroller. At the top of the cliff was a hotel—a future hotel, rather—unfinished, its walls raw white, its windows sealed by planks and cardboard.

Maigret calmly pushed open the gate of the gray stone house, Dr. Michoux's. When he was on the doorstep and reaching for the knob, Inspector Leroy murmured: "We have no warrant! Don't you think . . . ?"

Once again, Maigret shrugged. On the path, they could see the deep tracks left by the yellow dog's paws. There were also other prints: those of enormous feet, in hobnailed boots—size fourteen at least!

The knob turned. The door opened as if by magic, and on the carpet inside were the same muddy tracks, of the dog and of those amazing boots.

The house, elaborate in its architecture, was just as pretentious inside. Nothing but nooks and crannies everywhere, filled with couches, low bookcases, Breton closet-beds transformed into vitrines, little Turkish or Chinese tables, dozens of rugs and hangings. The place strained for a kind of folk-modern effect.

There were a few Breton landscapes, and some signed nude drawings with dedications on them: "To my good friend Michoux," "To the artist's friend."

The superintendent gazed sullenly at all the bric-a-brac, but the young Leroy was rather impressed by the false elegance.

Maigret opened doors, glanced into the rooms. Some were unfurnished. The plaster was barely dry on the walls.

Finally he pushed one door open with his foot and gave a grunt of satisfaction on seeing the kitchen. On the pine table stood two empty Bordeaux bottles.

A dozen cans had been roughly opened with a knife. The table was smeared with dirt and grease. Someone had eaten straight from the cans—herring in white wine, cold cassoulet, mushrooms, and apricots.

The floor was filthy. Scraps of meat lay around. There was a broken bottle of brandy, and the stench of alcohol mingled with that of the food.

Maigret looked at his companion with an odd smile. "Well, Leroy, do you suppose the doctor is the pig who eats like this?"

When the dumbfounded Leroy did not answer, he went on: "Not his mama, either, I hope! Or the maid. Look! You like prints. These are more like crusts of mud. That'll give you a perfect outline of the soles—size thirteen or fourteen, I'd say. And the dog's tracks too!"

He filled a new pipe, picked up some matches from a shelf. "Take whatever evidence there is to take in here. You've got a big job ahead of you. See you later!"

His hands in his pockets, the collar of his coat turned up, he went off along the White Sands beach.

When he stepped into the Admiral café, the first person he saw was Dr. Michoux, in his usual corner, still in his slippers, unshaven, his scarf around his neck.

Next to him sat Le Pommeret, turned out as meticulously as the night before. The two men watched silently as the superintendent approached.

It was the doctor who finally said, in a hoarse voice, "You know what I just heard? Servières has disappeared . . . His wife is going out of her mind . . . He left here last night, and nobody's seen him since."

Maigret gave a start, not because of this news, but because he had just caught sight of the yellow dog, stretched out at Emma's feet.

3

FEAR REIGNS IN CONCARNEAU

Le Pommeret had to confirm Michoux's story, for the pleasure of hearing himself talk:

"She came to my house a while ago begging me to look for him. Servières—his real name is Goyard—is an old friend . . ."

Maigret's gaze moved from the yellow dog to the door as it flew open for a newsboy, who entered like a gust of wind, and then to a headline in type big enough to read from across the room:

FEAR REIGNS IN CONCARNEAU

The subheads read:

> *New mystery daily*
> DISAPPEARANCE OF OUR COLLEAGUE JEAN
>   SERVIÈRES
> *Bloodstains in his car*
> WHOSE TURN NEXT?

Maigret caught the newsboy by the sleeve. "Have you sold a lot of those?"

"Ten times as many as on a regular day. There are three of us running them from the station."

Set free, the boy raced off along the quay calling, "*Brest Beacon*! Sensational issue!"

The superintendent hardly had time to start reading the article when Emma announced, "You're wanted on the phone."

It was the mayor's voice. He was furious. "Hello, superintendent! Are you behind this idiotic article? . . . And I didn't know a thing! I insist—do you hear me?—I insist on being the first person informed about what happens in this town. I'm the mayor! What is this story about the car? And this man with big feet? In the past half hour I've had over twenty phone calls from panicky people asking me if the news is true! . . . I repeat, from now on I want—"

Without turning a hair, Maigret hung up and returned to the café, where he sat and began to read. Michoux and Le Pommeret scanned a copy of the paper on the marble table.

Our esteemed colleague Jean Servières reported in these very pages the recent dramatic events in Concarneau. That was Friday. A respected businessman of that town, Monsieur Mostaguen, left the Admiral Hotel, stopped in the doorway of a vacant house to light a cigar, and was shot in the stomach by a bullet fired through the letter box in the door.

On Saturday, Superintendent Maigret, recently sent from Paris to head the Rennes mobile squad, arrived on the scene. This did not prevent a new drama from occurring.

Indeed, that very evening, a telephone call informed us that, as they were about to drink an aperitif, three prominent local figures—Messieurs Le Pommeret, Jean Servières, and Dr. Michoux—noticed that the Pernod served them contained a strong dose of strychnine.

Then this morning, Sunday, Jean Servières's empty car was found near the Saint-Jacques River. Its owner has not been seen since Saturday evening.

The front seat is stained with blood. One window is shattered, and all the evidence suggests that a struggle took place.

Three days: three incidents! No wonder terror is beginning to rule Concarneau, as the anguished citizens wonder who the next victim will be.

The public is particularly disturbed by the mysterious presence of a yellow dog, which no one knows, which seems to have no master, and which reappears with each new misfortune.

Is it true that this dog has shown the police a real trail? Are they not looking for a person, still unidentified, who has left curious tracks—tracks of feet far larger than average—in several places?

A madman? A drifter? Is he the perpetrator of all these crimes? Whom will he attack tonight?

He will certainly meet opposition from now on, be-

cause the frightened citizenry will be armed and ready
to shoot at the slightest alarm.

Meanwhile, today, Sunday, the town is deathly still,
and its mood recalls that of towns in northeast France
after an air-raid alert during the War.

Maigret stared out through the windowpanes. The rain
had let up, but the streets still flowed with black mud and
the wind still blew violently. The sky was a livid gray.

People were coming out of Mass. Almost all of them
carried a copy of the *Brest Beacon*. Faces were turned
toward the Admiral Hotel, and several people quickened
their step as they passed.

There certainly was something dead about the town.
But wasn't that true on any Sunday morning? The telephone rang again. Emma could be heard answering. "I
don't know, sir. I haven't heard. Do you want me to get the
superintendent? . . . Hello! Hello! . . . They hung up!"

"Who was that?" growled Maigret.

"A Paris newspaper, I think. They asked if there were
any new victims . . . They reserved a room."

"Call the *Brest Beacon* for me."

While he waited, he paced up and down, without a
glance at the doctor, who was huddling in his chair, or at
Le Pommeret, who was contemplating the many rings on
his fingers.

"Hello! The *Brest Beacon*? Superintendent Maigret
here. The editor, please . . . Hello—is that the editor? Good!
Would you tell me what time your rag came off press

this morning? . . . Nine thirty, eh? Who did the piece on the business at Concarneau? . . . Ah, no, seriously! . . . Really? The article just turned up in a sealed envelope? . . . Unsigned? . . . So, then, you publish whatever material you get, name or no name, just like that? . . . Well, my respects!"

He tried to go out to the quay, but found the door locked. "What does this mean?" he asked Emma, looking straight into her eyes.

"The doctor insisted . . ."

Maigret stared at Michoux, whose expression was more evasive than ever, shrugged his shoulders, and went out through the hotel door. Most of the shops had their shutters closed. People in Sunday clothes hurried by.

Beyond the harbor, where boats were tugging at their moorings, Maigret found the mouth of the Saint-Jacques River. It was at the very edge of town, where houses thinned out and shipyards took over. Several half-finished vessels stood on the ways. Old boats lay rotting in the mud.

A stone bridge crossed the river where it emptied into the harbor, and there a group of inquisitive people stood around a small car.

The nearby wharves were blocked by construction, so Maigret had to make a detour to get there. From the looks he received on the way, he realized that everyone already knew who he was. He saw anxious people talking quietly near the doorways of the closed shops.

Finally, he reached the car abandoned at the side of the

road. He pulled the door open brusquely, scattering shards
of glass, and easily made out the brown streaks on the seat
cover.

The onlookers, mainly street boys and overdressed
young yokels, crowded around him.

"Monsieur Servières's house?"

A dozen people led him to it. It was a quarter of a mile
away, rather secluded—a middle-class house with a garden. His escort stopped at the gate. Maigret rang the bell,
and was let in by a little maid who looked upset.

"Is Madame Servières here?"

She was already opening the door to the dining room.

"Oh, superintendent! . . . Do you think he's been killed?
I'm going out of my mind! I . . ."

She was a handsome woman, about forty, and had the
look of a competent housewife, an impression confirmed
by the tidiness of her home.

"You haven't seen your husband since—"

"He was home for dinner last night. I could see that he
was worried, but he didn't want to say anything to me . . .
He'd left the car at the gate, which meant that he was
going out again that night . . . to play his regular card
game at the Admiral. I asked him if he'd be late coming
home . . . At ten o'clock, I went to bed. I was awake a long
time. I heard the clock strike eleven, then half past. But he
often came home very late . . . I must have fallen asleep finally. I woke up in the middle of the night, and was upset
not to find him beside me . . . Then I decided that someone
must have taken him along to Brest. There's not much go-

ing on here, so sometimes he . . . I couldn't get back to sleep. From five o'clock on, I was up and watching out of the window. He doesn't like me to wait up for him, and even less for me to check on him . . . At nine, I ran over to Monsieur Le Pommeret's . . . I was coming back another way when I saw people gathered round his car . . . Tell me! Why would anyone want to kill him? He's the kindest man on earth . . . I'm sure he has no enemies."

A small group still clustered at the gate.

"They say there are bloodstains! I saw people reading a newspaper, but no one showed it to me."

"Did your husband have much money on him?"

"I don't think so . . . The same as usual—three or four hundred francs."

Maigret promised to keep her informed, even took the trouble to comfort her with a few vague remarks. The scent of roast lamb came from the kitchen. The maid, in her white apron, led him back to the door.

The superintendent had gone no more than a hundred yards when a man approached him eagerly. "Excuse me, superintendent. Let me introduce myself: Monsieur Dujardin, teacher. For the past hour, people—mostly the parents of my students—have been coming to ask me if there's any truth to what the newspaper says. Some of them want to know whether they have the right to shoot if they see that man with the big feet—"

Maigret was no angel of patience. Shoving his hands into his pockets, he snarled, "Leave me alone!"

And he headed back to the center of town.

It was idiotic! He'd never known anything like it. It made him think of a storm in a film. You see a cheerful street, a calm sky. Then a cloud slides over the scene and blocks the sun. A violent wind sweeps through the street. Murky lighting, banging shutters, whirling dust, large drops. And suddenly the street is under a lashing rain, under a theatrical sky.

Concarneau was changing before his eyes. The piece in the *Brest Beacon* was only the beginning. For some time now, word of mouth had far outstripped the written version.

And besides it was Sunday. The people in the town had time on their hands. You could see them deciding, for their walk, to go take a look at Jean Servières's car, near which two policemen had been posted. The idlers hung around for an hour or so, listening to the interpretations of the better informed.

When Maigret got back to the Admiral Hotel, the proprietor, in his chef's toque, clutched nervously at his sleeve. "I've got to talk to you, superintendent . . . This is becoming impossible."

"Just give me some lunch."

"But—"

Maigret, in a temper, sat down in a corner and ordered. "Bring me a beer! . . . Have you seen my inspector?"

"He went out. I think he was called over to the mayor's house . . . Someone just telephoned again from Paris. A newspaper has reserved two rooms, for a reporter and a photographer."

"Where's the doctor?"

"He's upstairs. He told us not to let anyone up."

"And Monsieur Le Pommeret?"

"He's just left."

The yellow dog was gone. Several young fellows, flowers in their buttonholes, hair slicked down with pomade, were seated around the tables, but they were not drinking the lemonades they had ordered. They had come to watch, and they were visibly proud of themselves for their boldness.

"Come here, Emma."

There was an instinctive rapport between the waitress and the superintendent. She approached readily and let him draw her into the corner.

"You're sure the doctor never went out last night?"

"I swear I didn't sleep in his room."

"So he might have gone out?"

"I don't think so. He's afraid . . . I told you he made me lock the door to the quay this morning."

"How come that yellow dog knows you?"

"I don't know. I've never seen him before . . . He comes, he goes . . . I wonder who feeds him."

"Has he been gone long?"

"I wasn't paying attention."

Inspector Leroy came back in a nervous state. "You know, superintendent, the mayor is furious . . . And he's a very influential man! He told me he's a cousin of the Minister of Justice. He claims all we're doing is churning things up and throwing the town into a panic . . . He wants us to arrest someone, anyone, to calm people down.

I promised him I'd talk to you about it. He kept telling me our careers—yours and mine, that is—are in jeopardy."

Maigret scraped serenely at the bowl of his pipe.

"What are you going to do?" asked Leroy.

"Nothing at all."

"But—"

"You're young, Leroy! . . . Did you pick up any worthwhile evidence at the doctor's house?"

"I've sent everything to the laboratory—the glasses, the cans, the knife. I even made a plaster cast of the footprints, the man's and the dog's. That was hard, because the plaster they've got here is very poor quality . . . Do you have any ideas?"

By way of answer, Maigret pulled a notebook from his pocket. The inspector, more baffled than ever, read:

Ernest Michoux *(called Doctor)*: *Son of small manufacturer in Seine-et-Oise who was deputy from that district for one term. And then went bankrupt. Father dead. Mother a schemer. Tried, with son, to establish property development at Juan-les-Pins. Complete failure. Started again at Concarneau. Set up a corporation, trading on dead husband's name. Invested no capital herself. Now trying to get town and district to underwrite development costs.*

Ernest Michoux was married, then divorced. His former wife married a notary in Lille.

Degenerate type. Has difficulty paying bills.

The inspector looked at his chief as if to say, "Meaning?"
Maigret showed him the next entry:

Yves Le Pommeret: *Prominent family. Brother
Arthur runs biggest canning plant in Concarneau.
Minor aristocracy. Yves the playboy of the family.
Never worked. Long ago ran through most of his
money in Paris. Came back to live in Concarneau
when he was down to twenty thousand francs a year.
Manages to come across as gentry even if he does
polish his own shoes. Many affairs with working
girls. A few scandals hushed up. Hunts at all the big
estates in the neighborhood. Big shot. Through
connections got himself named vice-consul for
Denmark. Pulling strings now for Légion d'Honneur.
Sometimes borrows from brother to pay his debts.*

Jean Servières *(pseudonym for Jean Goyard): Born
in Morbihan. Longtime journalist in Paris,
manager of little theaters, etc. Came into small
inheritance and settled in Concarneau. Married
former usherette who'd been his mistress for fifteen
years. Middle-class household. Occasional flings in
Brest and Nantes. Lives off little investments more
than off newspaper work, but very proud of latter.
Decorated by Academy.*

"I don't understand," stammered the inspector.
"Of course not. Give me your notes."

"But . . . who told you I . . ."

"Let's see them."

The superintendent's notebook was a cheap little pad of graph paper with an oilcloth cover. Inspector Leroy's was a loose-leaf daybook in a steel binder.

His manner paternal, Maigret read:

1. Matter of Mostaguen: *The bullet that hit the wine dealer was certainly intended for someone else. As there was no way to foresee that anyone would stop at that doorway, the real target must have been expected there, but never came, or came too late.*

Unless the purpose was to terrorize the population. The murderer knows Concarneau intimately. (Neglected to analyze cigarette ashes found in hallway.)

2. Matter of poisoned Pernod: *In wintertime, the Admiral café is empty almost all day. Anyone who knew this could enter and put poison in the bottles. In two bottles. Thus it was aimed specifically at the drinkers of Pernod and calvados. (Note, however, that the doctor spotted, in time and easily, the grains of white powder floating on the liquid.)*

3. Matter of yellow dog: *He knows the Admiral café. He has a master. But who? Seems to be at least five years old.*

4. Matter of Servières: *Determine by handwriting analysis who sent article to* Brest Beacon.

Maigret smiled, handed the book back to his companion, and remarked: "Very good, my boy."

Then, with an irritable glance at the gawkers' silhouettes beyond the green windows, he added, "Let's go and eat!"

A little later, when they were in the dining room, along with the traveling salesman who had arrived that morning, Emma informed them that Dr. Michoux was feeling worse and had asked for a light meal to be sent to his room.

_____

That afternoon the Admiral café was like a cage in the zoo, what with sightseers filing past its small dim windows in their Sunday best. They then headed toward the far end of the harbor to the next attraction—Servières's car, still guarded by two policemen.

The mayor phoned three times from his sumptuous house at White Sands. "Have you made an arrest?"

Maigret barely bothered to answer.

The young crowd, those from eighteen to twenty-five, invaded the café. Noisy groups took over tables and ordered drinks, which they never touched. They weren't in the café more than five minutes before their jokes petered out, their laughter died down, and awkwardness gave way to bluffing. And one by one they left.

The difference in the town was more apparent when it came time to light the streetlamps. It was four o'clock. Ordinarily at that hour the streets would still be busy. That evening, they were deserted, and deathly silent. It was as if the strollers had passed the word. In less than a quarter of an hour the streets had emptied, and when footsteps sounded, they were the hurried ones of someone anxious to get to the shelter of home.

Emma leaned on her elbows at the till. The proprietor went back and forth between the kitchen and the café, where Maigret stubbornly refused to listen to his lamentations.

Ernest Michoux came downstairs at about 4:30, still in slippers. Stubble covered his cheeks. His cream silk scarf was stained with sweat.

"Ah, you're here, superintendent!" The fact seemed to comfort him. "And your inspector?"

"I sent him off to look around town."

"The dog?"

"Hasn't been seen since this morning."

The floor was gray, the marble of the tables a harsh white veined with blue. Through the windows, the glowing Old Town clock was dimly visible, now showing ten minutes to five.

"We still don't know who wrote that article? . . ."

The newspaper lay on the table. By this point only one headline stood out:

WHOSE TURN NEXT?

The telephone jangled. Emma answered. "No . . . Nothing . . . I don't know anything."

"Who was it?" Maigret asked.

"Another Paris paper. They said their reporters are arriving by car."

She had hardly finished the sentence when the phone rang again.

"It's for you, superintendent."

The doctor, pale as a ghost, kept his eyes on Maigret.

"Hello! Who's there?"

"It's Leroy . . . I'm over in the Old Town, near the channel inlet. There's been a shooting here . . . A shoemaker saw the yellow dog from his window and—"

"Dead?"

"Wounded! Badly. In the hindquarters. The animal can barely drag himself along. People don't dare go near him . . . I'm calling from a café. The dog is in the middle of the street—I can see him through the window. He's howling . . . What should I do?" And despite his effort to keep calm, the inspector's voice was tense, as if the wounded yellow dog were some supernatural creature. "There are people at every window . . . What should I do, superintendent? Finish him off?"

His color leaden, the doctor stood behind Maigret, asking fearfully, "What is it? . . . What's he saying?"

And the superintendent saw Emma leaning on the counter, her expression blank.

4

FIELD HEADQUARTERS

Maigret crossed the drawbridge, passed through the Old Town ramparts, and turned down a crooked, poorly lighted street. What the people of Concarneau call "the closed town"—the old section still surrounded by its walls—is one of the most densely settled parts.

As the superintendent advanced, however, he entered a zone of ever more ambiguous silence, the silence of a crowd hypnotized by a spectacle, and trembling with fear or impatience. Here and there, a few isolated voices, those of adolescents determined to sound bold, could be heard.

One last bend in the street and he reached the scene: a narrow lane, with people at all the windows, their rooms lit with oil lamps; a glimpse of beds; a group of people blocking the way, and, beyond, a large clearing, from which came the sound of hoarse breathing.

Maigret pushed through the spectators, mostly youngsters, who were surprised by his arrival. Two of them were still throwing stones at the dog. Their companions tried to stop them, saying, "Watch out!"

One of the boys flushed to the ears when Maigret shoved him to the left and strode toward the wounded animal. The silence then took on a different character. It was clear that a few moments earlier an unwholesome frenzy had been driving the crowd, except for one old woman, who cried from her window:

"It's shameful! You should haul them all in, superintendent. The whole bunch of them were torturing that poor creature . . . And I know perfectly well why. Because they're afraid of him!"

The shoemaker-gunman withdrew sheepishly into his shop. Maigret leaned down to stroke the dog's head; the animal gave him a look that was more puzzled than grateful. Inspector Leroy came out of the café from which he had telephoned. People began reluctantly to move away.

"Someone get a wheelbarrow."

Windows were closing one after another, but inquisitive shadows hovered behind the curtains. The dog was filthy, his dense coat matted with blood. His belly was muddy, his nose dry and burning. Now that someone was showing kindness, he took heart and stopped trying to creep along the ground through the dozens of large stones that lay around him.

"Where should we take him, superintendent?"

"To the hotel . . . Easy there . . . Put some straw under him."

The procession could have looked ridiculous. Instead, by some eerie effect of the anguish that had grown steadily stronger since morning, it was stirring. With an old man pushing it, the wheelbarrow bounced over the cobblestones of the twisting street and onto the drawbridge. No one dared follow it. The yellow dog panted hard, an occasional spasm stiffening all four legs.

Maigret noticed an unfamiliar car parked opposite the Admiral Hotel. He pushed open the café door and found the atmosphere transformed.

A man squeezed past him, saw the dog being lifted out of the wheelbarrow, aimed a camera at the animal, and set off a magnesium flash. Another, dressed in plus fours and a red sweater, with notebook in hand, touched the visor of his cap.

"Superintendent Maigret? Vasco, from the *Journal.* I've just got here, and already I've been lucky enough to meet Mister . . ." He indicated Michoux, who was in his corner, slouching against the moleskin banquette. "The *Petit Parisien* is right behind. They broke down about ten kilometers back."

"Where do you want the dog?" Emma asked the superintendent.

"Isn't there a spot for him in the hotel?"

"Yes, near the courtyard . . . a porch where we store empty bottles."

"Leroy! Phone a vet."

An hour earlier, the place was deserted, seething with silence. Now, the photographer, in an off-white trench coat, was shoving tables and chairs around and yelling, "Wait a minute! Hold it, please! Turn the dog's head this way . . ." And the magnesium flared.

"Le Pommeret?" Maigret asked Dr. Michoux.

"He left not long after you did . . . The mayor phoned again. I think he may be on his way over . . ."

By nine that evening, the place had become a sort of military headquarters. Two more reporters had arrived. One was working on his story at a table toward the back. From time to time the photographer came down from his room. "You wouldn't have any rubbing alcohol? I've absolutely got to have it to dry my film . . . The dog looks terrific! . . . Did you say there's a pharmacy nearby? . . . Closed? Doesn't matter."

At the hall phone, a reporter was dictating his story, in an offhand voice:

"Maigret, yes—*M* as in Maurice, *A* as in Arthur . . . Yes. *I* as in Isidore . . . Take down all the names first . . . Michoux—*M, I, choux,* as in *choucroute* . . . No, no, not like *pou*. Now wait—I'm going to give you the headlines . . . Will this go on page one? . . . Absolutely! Tell the boss it's got to go on the front page . . ."

Feeling lost, Inspector Leroy kept looking at Maigret as if to get his bearings. In a corner, the lone traveling salesman was preparing his next day's route with the help of the regional directory. Now and then he would call over to Emma.

"Chauffier's . . . is that a big hardware outlet? . . . Thanks."

The vet had removed the bullet and set the dog's

hindquarters in a cast. "These animals, it takes a lot to kill them!"

Emma had spread an old blanket over straw on the blue granite floor of the porch that gave onto both the courtyard and the cellar stairway. The dog lay there, all alone, inches from a scrap of meat he never touched.

The mayor arrived by car. He was a very well-groomed elderly man with a small white goatee; his gestures were curt. His eyebrows rose as he entered and noticed the atmosphere of a guardroom—or, more precisely, a field headquarters.

"Who are these gentlemen?"

"Reporters from Paris."

The mayor was very touchy. "Wonderful! So tomorrow the whole country will be talking about this idiotic business! . . . You still haven't found out anything?"

"The investigation is still going on!" growled Maigret, as if to say, "None of your business!"

For the atmosphere was really tense. Everyone's nerves were on edge.

"And you, Michoux, you're not going home?" The mayor's look of contempt made clear that he thought the doctor a coward.

"At this rate," he said, turning back to Maigret, "there'll be full-scale panic within the next twenty-four hours . . . What we need—as I told you before—is an arrest, no matter who." He emphasized his last words with a glance at Emma. "I know I have no authority to give you orders . . . As for the local police, you're ignoring them completely . . .

But I'll tell you this: one more crime, just one, and we'll have a catastrophe on our hands. People are expecting trouble. Shops that on any other Sunday stay open till nine at night have already closed their shutters . . . That idiotic piece in the *Brest Beacon* terrified the public . . ."

The mayor, who had not taken his bowler off his head, now pulled it down farther as he left, saying, "I'll thank you to keep me informed, superintendent . . . And I remind you that whatever happens now is your responsibility."

"A beer, Emma!" Maigret snapped.

There was no way to keep the reporters from descending on the Admiral Hotel, or from installing themselves in the café, telephoning and filling the place with their noisy commotion. They demanded ink, paper. They interrogated Emma, whose poor face looked constantly alarmed.

Outside, the night was dark, with a beam of moonlight that heightened the melodrama of the cloudy sky instead of brightening it. And there was the mud, which clung to every shoe, since paved streets were still unknown in Concarneau.

"Did Le Pommeret tell you he was coming back?" Maigret suddenly asked Michoux.

"Yes. He went home for dinner."

"His address?" asked a reporter who had nothing else to do.

The doctor gave it to him, as the superintendent shrugged and pulled Leroy off into a corner.

"Did you get the original manuscript of this morning's article?"

"I just got it. It's in my room . . . The handwriting is disguised. It must have come from someone who thought they'd know his writing."

"No postmark?"

"No. The envelope was dropped in the newspaper's box. It says 'Special Rush' on it . . ."

"Which means that at eight this morning, at the latest, someone knew about Jean Servières's disappearance, knew that the car was, or would be, abandoned near the Saint-Jacques River, and that there would be bloodstains on the seat . . . And that same someone also knew that we'd discover the tracks of an unknown man with big feet . . ."

"It's amazing!" sighed the inspector. "But about those fingerprints—I wired them off to the Quai des Orfèvres. They've already checked the files and called me back. The prints don't match those of any known offender."

There was no doubt about it, the tension was getting to Leroy. But the person most thoroughly infected, so to speak, by that virus was Ernest Michoux, who looked even more colorless in contrast to the newspapermen's sporty clothes, easygoing style, and assurance.

He had no idea what to do with himself. Maigret asked him: "You're not going up to bed?"

"Not yet . . . I never fall asleep before one in the morning . . ." He forced a feeble smile, which showed two gold teeth. "Frankly, what do you think?"

The lighted clock in the Old Town tolled ten. The superintendent was called to the telephone. It was the mayor.

"Still nothing?" It sounded as if he, too, was expecting trouble.

But, actually, wasn't Maigret expecting trouble himself? Frowning, he went out to visit the yellow dog. The animal had dozed off; now, without alarm, he opened one eye to watch Maigret approach. The superintendent stroked his head, pushed a handful of straw beneath his front legs.

He felt the proprietor come up behind him.

"Do you suppose those newspaper people will be staying long? . . . Because if they are, I ought to think about supplies. The market opens at six tomorrow morning . . ."

For anyone not used to Maigret, it could be unsettling to see his large eyes stare blankly at you, as now, then hear him mutter something incomprehensible and move on as if you were not worth noticing.

The reporter from the *Petit Parisien* returned, shaking his dripping raincoat.

"Well! It's raining?" someone asked. "What's new, Groslin?"

The young man's eyes sparkled as he spoke quietly to his photographer, then picked up the telephone.

"*Petit Parisien,* operator . . . Press service—urgent! What? You have a tie-line to Paris? . . . Well then, hurry . . . Hello! *Petit Parisien*? Mademoiselle Germaine? Give me the copy-taking department. This is Groslin!"

His tone was impatient. And he darted a challenging look at the colleagues listening to him. Passing by, Maigret stopped to listen.

"Hello, is that you, Mademoiselle Jeanne? . . . This is a rush! There's still time to make a few of the out-of-town runs. The other papers will only be able to get it into their Paris editions. Tell the copydesk to rewrite what I give you; I don't have time. Here we go:

"The Concarneau Case. Our predictions were correct: another crime . . . Hello? Yes, *crime*! A man's been killed. Is that better?"

Everyone was silent. Spellbound, the doctor drew close to the reporter as he went on, excited, triumphant.

"First Monsieur Mostaguen, then the newspaperman Jean Servières, and now Monsieur Le Pommeret! . . . Yes, I spelled the name earlier. He was just found dead in his room . . . at home. No wound. His muscles are rigid. All evidence points to poisoning. Wait—end with: Terror reigns . . . Yes! Rush this to the managing editor . . . I'll call back in a while to dictate a piece for the Paris edition, but the information has to get to the out-of-town desks now."

He hung up, mopped his face, and threw a jubilant look around the room.

The telephone was ringing again.

"Hello. Superintendent? We've been trying to get through to you for a quarter of an hour. I'm calling from Monsieur Le Pommeret's house . . . Hurry! He's dead!" And the voice repeated, in a wail, "Dead!"

Maigret looked around. Empty glasses stood on almost every table. Emma, her face drained, followed his eyes.

"Nobody touch a single glass or bottle!" he ordered. "You hear me, Leroy? Don't leave here."

Sweat dripping from his brow, the doctor snatched off his scarf; at his skinny neck, his shirt was fastened by a toggle stud.

————

By the time Maigret reached Le Pommeret's apartment, a doctor from next door had already made the initial examination.

A woman of about fifty was there. She was the owner of the building, the person who had telephoned.

It was a pretty house of gray stone, facing the sea. Every twenty seconds, the glowing brush of the lighthouse beacon set the windows on fire. There was a balcony with a flagstaff and a shield bearing the Danish coat of arms.

Outside, five people watched wordlessly as the superintendent went in.

The body lay on the reddish carpet of a studio crowded with worthless knickknacks. On the walls were publicity shots of actresses, framed pictures clipped from sexy magazines, and a few signed photos of women.

Le Pommeret's shirt was pulled out of his trousers, his shoes were still crusted with mud.

"Strychnine," said the doctor. "At least so far I'd swear to that. Look at his eyes. And notice especially how rigid the body is. The death throes took over half an hour. Maybe more . . ."

"Where were you?" Maigret asked the landlady.

"Downstairs. I sublet the whole second floor to Monsieur Le Pommeret, and he took his meals at my place . . .

He came home for dinner around eight o'clock. He ate almost nothing. I remember he said there was something wrong with the electricity, but the lights seemed perfectly normal to me. He said he'd be going out again, but that first he'd go up and take an aspirin, because his head felt heavy . . ."

The superintendent looked questioningly at the doctor.

"That's it! The early symptoms."

"Which appear how long after absorbing the poison?"

"That depends on the dose and on the person's constitution. Sometimes half an hour, sometimes two hours."

"And death?"

"Doesn't come until after general paralysis sets in. But there is local paralysis first. So he probably tried to call for help . . . He would have been lying on this couch . . ."

The couch that had earned Le Pommeret's place the name Turpitude Hall! Pornographic prints crowded the walls around the couch. A night-light gave off a rosy glow.

"He'd have gone into convulsions. Like an attack of delirium tremens . . . He died on the floor."

Maigret walked to the door as a photographer started to come in and slammed it in the man's face.

"Le Pommeret left the Admiral a little after seven o'clock," Maigret calculated. "He'd had a brandy-and-water . . . A quarter of an hour later, he drank and ate something here . . . From what you say about the way strychnine works, it's just as possible he was poisoned back there as here . . ."

Abruptly, he went downstairs, where the landlady was crying, with three of her neighbors around her.

"The dishes, the glasses from dinner?"

It took her a moment to understand what Maigret wanted. By the time she replied, he had already looked into the kitchen and seen a basin of warm water, clean plates and glasses laid out to the right, dirty to the left.

"I was just washing up when . . ."

A local policeman arrived.

"Watch the house," Maigret told him. "Put everyone out except the landlady . . . and no reporters, no photographers! Nobody is to touch a glass or a plate."

It was five hundred yards, through the downpour, to the hotel. The town was dark except for two or three distant lighted windows. Then on the square, at the corner by the quay, the Admiral Hotel's three square windows shone out, though their green panes made the place look like a huge aquarium.

As Maigret drew near, he heard voices, the telephone ringing, and then the roar of a car starting up.

"Where are you heading?" he asked the reporter in it.

"The phone is tied up. I'm going to look for another one. In ten minutes it'll be too late to make my Paris edition."

Standing in the café, Inspector Leroy looked like a teacher monitoring prep. Men were writing without pause. The traveling salesman watched, bewildered but excited by a scene that was entirely new to him.

Glasses still stood on the tables—stemware for aperitifs, beer mugs slick with foam, small liqueur glasses.

"When did you last clear the tables?"

Emma thought back. "I can't say exactly. I picked up some glasses as I went by. Others are left from this afternoon."

"What about Monsieur Le Pommeret's?"

"What did he drink, Dr. Michoux?" she asked.

It was Maigret who answered: "A brandy-and-water."

She looked at the saucers, one after another, checking the prices on them. "This one says six francs . . . But I served one of those men a whiskey, and that's the same price . . . Maybe that glass over there? . . . Maybe not . . ."

The photographer, sticking to business, was taking pictures of the glassware spread on the marble tabletops.

"Go and get the pharmacist," the superintendent ordered Leroy.

And from then on it was a long night of glasses and plates. Some were brought from the vice-consul of Denmark's house. The reporters made themselves at home in the pharmacist's laboratory, and one of them, a former medical student, even helped out with the analyses.

The mayor, by telephone, merely remarked sharply: "Entirely your responsibility."

The proprietor suddenly appeared and asked, "What's become of the dog?"

The place where he had been lying on straw was empty. The yellow dog was incapable of walking, or even crawling, because of the cast immobilizing his hindquarters, but he had vanished.

The glasses revealed nothing.

"Monsieur Le Pommeret's may have been washed already . . . I can't tell in all this commotion!" said Emma.

At his landlady's, too, half the dishes had already been rinsed in warm water.

Ernest Michoux, his face ashen, was more disturbed over the dog's disappearance. "Someone came through the courtyard and took him! There's a way through to the quay, a kind of alleyway . . . That gate has to be sealed, superintendent! Or else . . . To think that someone got in without anybody knowing! And then left with that animal in his arms!"

It looked as if the doctor didn't dare move from his corner, as if he was keeping as far as possible from the doors.

5

THE MAN AT CABÉLOU

It was eight in the morning. Maigret, who had never gone to bed, had taken a bath and was now shaving at a mirror dangling from the window latch.

It had turned colder, and the rain was mixed with sleet. A reporter was waiting downstairs for the Paris newspapers. The 7:30 train had sounded its whistle, and soon the newsboys would arrive with the latest sensational issues.

Below the superintendent's window, the square overflowed with the weekly market. Yet the usual liveliness of a market was missing: people talked in low voices; farmers looked uneasy.

In the open square stood some fifty stalls, piled with butter, eggs, vegetables, pairs of braces, silk stockings. To the right, carts of all kinds were lined up. And the whole scene was dominated by the winglike movement of the broad white lace headdresses of the local women.

Maigret noticed that something special was happening when a part of the market scene changed its look; people had drawn together and were staring in the same direction. Because his window was closed he heard only a jumbled murmur.

He looked farther off. On the quay, a few fishermen had been loading empty baskets and nets onto their boats. Suddenly they had stopped, and now made way for two local policemen, who were leading a prisoner toward the Town Hall.

One of the policemen was young, still beardless. His face radiated eager innocence. The other had a large mahogany-colored mustache, and his heavy eyebrows gave him an almost ferocious look.

In the market, all chatter had stopped, as the crowd watched the three men approach. Some pointed to the handcuffs that bound the prisoner's wrists to those of his captors.

The man was a colossus! His forward pitch made his shoulders look even broader. As he dragged his feet through the mud, he seemed to be towing the officers along in his wake.

He was wearing an unprepossessing old jacket, and his bare head bristled with thick hair, short and dark.

The waiting reporter darted up the hotel stairs, rattled a door, and shouted to his sleeping photographer: "Benoît! Benoît! Quick, get up! You'll miss a fantastic shot!"

He didn't know how right he was. For as Maigret, his eyes never leaving the square, wiped the last traces of shaving soap from his cheeks and reached for his jacket, a truly extraordinary thing happened.

The crowd had quickly closed around the policemen and their prisoner. Suddenly, the captive, who must have been waiting for the chance, gave a violent jerk of his wrists.

The superintendent saw the puny ends of chain dangling

from the policemen's hands. The man plunged through the crowd. A woman fell down. People scattered. A stall collapsed on its mounds of butter. Before anyone recovered from the surprise, the prisoner had darted into an alleyway, twenty yards from the Admiral, that went alongside the vacant house from which the bullet had spat forth on Friday.

The younger policeman nearly fired, but hesitated, then ran off, with his gun at the ready. Maigret was afraid there might be an accident.

But the young man was brave enough to dart alone into the alley. And since Maigret knew the neighborhood now, he finished dressing without haste.

It would take a miracle to catch the fellow. The narrow passage, six feet wide, had two sharp doglegs. Twenty houses, facing the quay or the square, had their back entries on the alley. There were storage sheds as well, a marine supply yard, a cannery warehouse, a whole tangle of odd buildings, nooks and crannies, and roofs within easy reach. They all made pursuit almost impossible.

The crowd was keeping its distance now. Red with anger, the woman who had been knocked down was shaking her fist in all directions as tears trickled down her chin.

The photographer darted from the hotel, a trench coat over his pajamas, his feet bare.

———

Half an hour later, just after the police lieutenant had sent his men to search the neighboring house, the mayor arrived. He found Maigret settled in the café with the young policeman, busily devouring toast.

The town's leading magistrate shook with indignation. "I warned you, superintendent, that I would hold you responsible for . . . for . . . But you don't seem to care! I'm going to send a telegram to the Minister of the Interior, to inform him of . . . of . . . and to ask him . . . Have you any idea what's happening out there? People are fleeing their homes. A helpless old man is howling with fear because he's stuck on the third floor. People think they're seeing the criminal everywhere!"

Maigret turned and saw Ernest Michoux huddling close behind him like a frightened child, trying to take up no more space than a ghost.

"You'll notice that it was the local police—just ordinary policemen—who arrested him, whereas . . ."

"You still insist that I make an arrest?"

"What do you mean? Are you claiming you can lay hands on the fugitive?"

"You asked me yesterday to make an arrest, any arrest . . ."

The reporters were outside, helping the police in their search. The café was practically empty. There had been no time to clean it up, though, and an acrid odor of stale tobacco smoke hung in the air. The floor was covered with cigarette butts, spittle, sawdust, and broken glass.

The superintendent drew a blank arrest warrant from his wallet. "Say the word, *Monsieur le Maire,* and I'll—"

"I'd be curious to know whom you would arrest!"

"Emma, pen and ink, please."

Maigret was drawing short puffs on his pipe. He heard the mayor mutter, just loud enough to be heard, "Bluffing!"

Unflustered, he wrote, in his usual large angular strokes: *Ernest Michoux, Director, White Sands Property Company.*

———

The scene was more comic than tragic. The mayor read the warrant upside down. Maigret said, "There you are! Since you insist, I'm arresting the doctor . . ."

Michoux looked at the two of them, gave the sickly smile of a man who cannot decide how to take a joke. But it was Emma the superintendent was watching—Emma, who walked toward the till and suddenly turned around, less pale than usual and unable to disguise a surge of joy.

"I suppose, superintendent, that you realize the gravity of—"

"It's my trade, *Monsieur le Maire.*"

"And the best you can do, after what's happened, is arrest a friend of mine—an associate, rather—and one of Concarneau's distinguished citizens?"

"Have you got a comfortable jail?"

During this conversation, Michoux seemed to be having a problem swallowing.

"Aside from the police station, in the Town Hall, there's only the police barracks, in the Old Town . . ."

Inspector Leroy had just come in. He gasped when Maigret said to him, in a perfectly natural voice: "Now,

Leroy, be so good as to escort the doctor to the police barracks. Discreetly. No need to handcuff him . . . Lock him up, and make sure he has everything he needs."

"It's utter madness!" babbled the doctor. "I don't understand what's going on . . . I . . . It's unheard of . . . It's an outrage!"

"Yes, indeed," Maigret muttered.

Turning to the mayor, he said: "I have no objection to continuing the search for your vagrant—that keeps the public busy. It might even be useful. But don't attach too much importance to his capture . . . Reassure people."

"You're aware that when the police caught him this morning they found a flick knife on him?"

"I'm not surprised."

Maigret was growing impatient. Standing up, he slipped on his heavy overcoat, turned up its velvet collar, and brushed his bowler hat on his sleeve.

"I'll see you later, *Monsieur le Maire*. I'll keep you informed. Another word of advice: try to keep people from talking too much to the reporters. When it comes right down to it, there's barely enough in all this to shake a stick at . . . Are you coming?" This question was addressed to the young policeman, who glanced at the mayor as if to say, "Excuse me, but I have to go along with him."

Inspector Leroy was circling the doctor like a man utterly perplexed by an unwieldy bundle.

Maigret tapped Emma on the cheek as he passed, and then crossed the square, unruffled by the curious stares. "This way?"

"Yes. We have to go round the harbor. It should take half an hour."

The fishermen were less interested than the townsfolk in the drama going on around the Admiral café. A dozen boats were making the most of the lull in the storm and sculling out to the harbor mouth to pick up the wind.

The policeman kept looking at Maigret like a pupil eager to please his teacher. "You know, the mayor played cards with the doctor at least twice a week. This must have given him a shock."

"What are people saying?"

"That depends. Ordinary folks—workers, fishermen—aren't too upset . . . In a way, they're even kind of glad about what's happening. The doctor, Monsieur Le Pommeret, and Monsieur Servières aren't very well thought of around here. Of course, they're important people, and nobody would dare say anything to them . . . Still, they overdid it, corrupting the girls from the canning plant . . . And in the summer it was worse, with their Paris friends. They were always drinking, making a racket in the streets at two in the morning, as if the town belonged to them. We got a lot of complaints . . . Especially about Monsieur Le Pommeret, who couldn't see anything in a skirt without getting carried away . . . It's sad to say, but things are slow at the cannery. There's a lot of unemployment. So, if you've got a little money . . . all those girls . . ."

"Well, in that case, who's upset?"

"The middle class. And the businessmen who rubbed shoulders with that bunch at the Admiral café . . . That was like the center of town, you know. Even the mayor went there . . ."

The man was flattered by Maigret's attention.

"Where are we?"

"We've just left town. From here on, the coast is pretty much deserted . . . just rocks, pine woods, and a few summer houses used by people from Paris . . . It's what we call Cabélou Point."

"What made you think of nosing around out here?"

"When you told me and my partner to look for a drifter who might be the owner of the yellow dog, we first searched the old boats in the inner harbor. Now and then we find a tramp there. Last year, a cutter burned up because someone made a fire to get warm and forgot to put it out."

"Find anything?"

"Nothing. It was my partner who thought of the old watchtower at Cabélou . . . We're just coming to it—that square stone structure on the last rocky point. It dates from the same time as the Old Town fortifications. Come this way . . . watch out for the muck . . . A very long time ago, a caretaker lived here, a kind of watchman, who signaled when boats passed. From it, you can see really far. It overlooks the Glénan Islands channel, the only opening to the sea. But it hasn't been manned for maybe fifty years."

Maigret stepped through an opening whose door had vanished, and entered a space with a beaten earth floor. On the ocean side, narrow slits gave a view out over the water. On the other side was a single window, without panes or a frame. On the stone walls were inscriptions cut by knifepoint; on the ground were dirty papers and all kinds of rubbish.

"For nearly fifteen years, a man lived here, all alone. Weak in the head—sort of a nature child. He slept over in that corner. Didn't mind the cold or the damp, or even the storms that flung spray in through the slits. He was a local oddity. In the summer, the Parisians would come to look at him, give him coins. A postcard peddler took a picture of him and sold it at the entrance . . . The man finally died, during the War. And no one ever bothered to clean the place up . . . Yesterday, my partner thought that if someone was hiding out around here, this might be the spot."

Maigret started up the narrow stone stairway cut right into the wall and reached the lookout, a granite tower open on all four sides, giving a view of the whole area.

"This was the watchtower. Before beacon lights were invented, they used to burn a fire here on the terrace . . . Anyhow, this morning very early, we came up here, me and my partner. We moved on tiptoe. And downstairs, right where the half-wit used to sleep, we saw a man snoring away—a giant! You could hear him breathing fifteen yards away. We managed to slip the handcuffs on him before he woke up."

They went back to the square room below, which was freezing cold from the wind.

"Did he struggle?"

"Not at all! My partner asked for his papers, and he

didn't answer . . . You never got a good look at him, did you? . . . He was stronger than the two of us together, so I never took my finger off the trigger of my revolver. What hands! Yours are big, but try to picture hands twice that big, with tattoos on them—"

"Did you see what they were?"

"All I could make out was an anchor, on the left hand, with the letters *S S* on both. There were some other complicated designs . . . maybe a snake . . . We didn't touch the mess lying around him. Look!"

There were bottles of good wine and expensive liquor, empty cans, and about twenty unopened ones. In the center of the room were the ashes of a fire and, nearby, a stripped lamb bone, chunks of bread, a few fish spines, a big scallop shell, and some lobster claws.

"Some feast, eh?" exclaimed the young policeman, who had probably never eaten such food. "This explains the complaints that have come in lately—a six-pound loaf stolen from the baker's, a basket of whiting that disappeared from a fishing boat, and the Prunier warehouse manager's claim that someone was swiping his lobsters during the night. We didn't pay much attention, because it was never very much."

Maigret was trying to work out how many days it would take a man with a big appetite to consume the amount of food indicated by the debris. "A week . . ." he murmured. "Yes—counting the lamb . . ."

Abruptly he asked, "What about the dog?"

"Yes. He wasn't here. There are plenty of paw prints on

the ground, but we didn't see the animal . . . You know, the mayor must be in a state over the doctor. I'd be surprised if he didn't wire Paris."

"The man was armed?"

"No. I was the one who searched him, while my partner, Piedboeuf, held on to the handcuffs and kept his gun on him. In one trouser pocket were roasted chestnuts, four or five of them. They must have come from the cart in front of the cinema on Friday and Saturday nights. Then there were a few coins, not even ten francs . . . A knife—but not a dangerous one; the kind sailors use to cut bread."

"He didn't say anything?"

"Not a word. We thought that he was simpleminded, like the old tenant . . . He stared at us like a bear would. He had a week's growth of beard and two broken teeth, right in the middle."

"What was he wearing?"

"I didn't notice . . . An old suit? I don't even know now if he was wearing a shirt or a sweater. He came along quietly . . . We were proud of our catch. He could have got away ten times before we made it back to town . . . So our guard was down when he gave that big yank that broke the chain between the cuffs. I thought my right wrist was broken. It still hurts . . . About Dr. Michoux . . ."

"What about him?"

"You know his mother's supposed to get back today or tomorrow . . . She's the widow of a deputy. They say she has a lot of influence. And she's a friend of the mayor's wife."

Maigret was gazing at the gray ocean through the slits. Small boats were tacking between Cabélou Point and a line of rocks marked by breaking surf; they came about and began to lay their nets less than a mile out.

"You really think it was the doctor who—"

"Let's go," said the superintendent.

The tide was coming in. When they left the tower, the water was starting to lap at the base. A hundred yards away, a boy was jumping from rock to rock as he checked lobster pots set in crevices. The young policeman could not keep quiet.

"The strange thing is that anyone would attack Monsieur Mostaguen. He's the best man in Concarneau; they even wanted to make him a district councillor . . . It seems he'll be all right, but they couldn't remove the bullet. So, for the rest of his life he'll be carrying a chunk of lead around in his belly! When you think that if he just hadn't felt like lighting a cigar . . ."

Rather than go around the harbor again, they crossed part of it on a ferry that shuttled to the Old Town.

A short distance from where the boys had been throwing stones at the dog the day before, Maigret noticed a wall with an enormous entryway surmounted by a flag and the words *National Police Barracks*.

He went in and crossed the courtyard of a building dating from Colbert's time. In an office there, Inspector Leroy was arguing with a police sergeant.

"About the doctor?" asked Maigret.

"Right! The sergeant won't hear of letting him get his meals sent in from outside."

"Unless you authorize it," the sergeant told Maigret. "And I'll need a signed document releasing me . . ."

The courtyard was as tranquil as a cloister. A fountain flowed with a cheerful gurgle.

"Where is he?"

"Down there, to the right. Push open that door. Then it's the second door along the corridor. Do you want me to go with you to open up? The mayor phoned to say we should treat the prisoner with the utmost consideration."

Maigret scratched his chin. Inspector Leroy and the policeman, about the same age, watched him with the same bashful curiosity.

A few minutes later, the superintendent stepped alone into a whitewashed cell that was no more dismal than any barracks room.

Michoux was seated at a small pine table. He stood up when Maigret entered, hesitated, then, with his eyes averted, began to speak:

"I assume, superintendent, that you're just staging this farce to head off another crime, to protect me from . . . from some attack . . ."

Maigret noticed that no one had relieved the doctor of his braces, his scarf, or his shoelaces, as regulations required. With the tip of his shoe he drew a chair over, sat down, filled his pipe, and said amiably: "Yes, indeed. But do sit down, doctor!"

6

A COWARD

"Are you superstitious, superintendent?"

Straddling his chair, his elbows on its back, Maigret pursed his lips in a way that might mean anything at all. The doctor had not sat down.

"I think we all are at certain times, or, if you like, when we're under pressure . . ." Michoux coughed into his handkerchief, looked at it worriedly, then went on.

"A week ago, I would have said I didn't believe in fortune-telling. And yet . . . It must be about five years ago now that I was having dinner with a few friends at the home of an actress in Paris. Over coffee, one of the guests suggested reading the cards . . . Well, do you know what he told me? Of course I laughed! I laughed all the more because it was so different from the usual line—blonde woman, old man who wishes you well, letter that comes from far away, and so on . . . To me, he said: 'You'll die a hideous death, a violent death. Beware of yellow dogs!'"

Michoux had not looked at the superintendent so far, but he glanced at him now. Maigret was placid—huge on the little chair, but a monument of placidity.

"That doesn't strike you as odd? . . . Through all the

years since, I never heard a word about a yellow dog. Then Friday there's a shooting. One of my friends is the victim. It could just as easily have been me who ducked into that doorway and got hit by the bullet. And suddenly a yellow dog turns up!

"Another friend disappears under weird circumstances. And the yellow dog is still stalking around.

"Yesterday, it was Le Pommeret's turn . . . The yellow dog again! . . . And you don't think I should be upset?"

He had never talked so much at once, and as he talked he became more confident. The only encouragement the superintendent offered was "Of course . . . of course."

"Isn't it disturbing? I realize I must have looked like a coward to you . . . Well, yes, I was afraid! It was a vague kind of fear, but it grabbed me by the throat from the minute the first attack . . . And then when the yellow dog came into the picture . . ."

He paced the cell with small steps, his eyes on the floor. Then his face came alive. "I almost asked you for protection, but I was afraid you would laugh. I was even more afraid of your contempt . . . Because strong men do feel contempt for cowards . . ."

His voice grew shrill. "And I admit it, superintendent: I am a coward! For the past four days I've been frightened—four days I've been sick with fright. It's no fault of mine! I know enough medicine to understand my own case.

"When I was born, they had to put me in an incubator. Growing up, I went through every single childhood disease.

"And when the war broke out, doctors who were examining five hundred men a day declared me fit for service and sent me to the front! Well, not only did I have weak lungs, scarred from old lesions, but two years earlier I'd had a kidney removed . . .

"I was terrified. Crazy with terror! Some hospital attendants picked me up after a shell exploded and buried me . . . And finally they realized that I didn't belong in the army.

"What I'm telling you may not be pretty. But I've been watching you. You look like a man who can understand . . .

"It's easy enough for strong people to despise cowards. But they ought to take the trouble to learn where the cowardice comes from . . .

"Look, I could see that you didn't think much of our group at the Admiral café. People told you that I sold land . . . a deputy's son, with a medical degree . . . and then all those evenings at a café table with those other failures.

"But what was I supposed to do? My parents were big spenders even though they weren't rich. That's not so rare in Paris. I was raised in luxury—all the great spas, and so on. Then my father died, and my mother started to dabble in the market and dream up schemes—just as much the great lady as ever, just as arrogant, but with creditors hounding her.

"So I helped her out. That was all I *could* do. This property development—nothing very impressive. And the

life here . . . Prominent citizens, oh, yes—but with something not quite solid about them.

"For three days now you've been watching me, and
I've been wishing I could talk to you openly . . . I used to
be married. My wife asked for a divorce because she
wanted a husband with more ambition . . .

"One kidney short—three or four days a week sick, exhausted, dragging myself from my bed to my chair . . ."

He sat down listlessly.

"Emma must have told you we've been lovers—mind-
lessly, you know? Just because sometimes you need to have
a woman . . . Not the sort of thing you tell everyone . . .

"At the Admiral café, I might have wound up going
mad. The yellow dog, Servières disappearing, the bloodstains in his car. And the worst was Le Pommeret's miser-
able death . . .

"Why him? Why not me? We were together two hours
earlier, at the same table, with the same glasses in front of
us . . . I had a premonition that if I left the hotel I'd be
next. I felt the circle tightening around me, that even in the
hotel, even locked in my room, danger was tracking me
down . . .

"I felt a kind of thrill when I saw you sign the warrant
for my arrest. And yet . . ." He looked at the walls around
him, at the window with three iron bars that opened on the
courtyard. "I'll have to move my bunk, push it into that
corner . . . How, yes, how in the world could someone tell
me about a yellow dog five years ago, when this dog here
was probably not even born? . . . I'm afraid, superinten-

dent! I admit that. I tell you I'm afraid! I don't care what people think when they hear I'm in jail. The only thing I care about is not dying. And someone's after me, someone I don't know, and who's already killed Le Pommeret, who probably killed Goyard, who shot Mostaguen ... Why? Tell me! Why? It must be some maniac. And they still haven't managed to wipe him out! He may be lurking nearby right now! He knows I'm here ... He'll come, with his awful dog that stares like a man!"

Maigret slowly stood up, knocked his pipe against his heel.

And the doctor repeated in a pitiful tone, "I know you think I'm a coward. It's going to be hell for me tonight, with this kidney ..."

Maigret stood there like the antithesis of the prisoner—of agitation, fever, sickness—the antithesis of that unwholesome and repellent terror. "Do you want me to send a doctor?"

"No! If I knew someone was supposed to come here, I'd be even more frightened. I'd be worried that *he* might turn up—the man with the dog, the maniac, the murderer."

Before long his teeth would start to chatter. "Do you think you'll arrest him? Or will you just kill him, like a mad dog? Because he *is* mad! Nobody kills the way he has for no reason!"

In another three minutes the doctor's frenzy would turn into a nervous breakdown. Maigret chose to leave, and the prisoner gazed after him, his head huddled between his shoulders, his eyelids red.

————

"Is that perfectly clear, sergeant? No one is to enter his cell except you, and you yourself are to take him his food and whatever else he needs. Meantime, take away anything he could use to kill himself with—his shoelaces, his tie. See that the courtyard is under surveillance day and night. And show consideration—the utmost consideration."

"Such a distinguished man!" sighed the sergeant. "You think he's the one who—"

"Who might be the next victim, yes. So you'll answer to me for his life!"

Maigret went off down the narrow street, splashing through the puddles. The whole town knew him by now. Curtains parted as he passed. Children broke off their games to watch him with timid respect.

He was crossing the drawbridge between the Old Town and the new when he ran into Inspector Leroy, who was looking for him.

"Anything new? I don't suppose they've laid hands on my bear, have they?"

"What bear?"

"The man with the big feet."

"No. The mayor gave orders to stop the search because it was upsetting the public. He placed a few policemen at strategic spots . . . But that's not what I wanted to talk to you about. It's the newspaperman, Goyard, Jean Servières. A traveling salesman who knows him just got into town, and he says he ran across him yesterday in Brest. Goyard pretended not to see him and walked off."

The inspector was surprised at how calmly Maigret took the news. "The mayor is convinced that the salesman was mistaken. He says there are plenty of short, fat men in any city. And you know what I heard him tell his deputy—talking low but hoping, I think, I'd overhear? Verbatim: 'Watch the superintendent take off on this false scent. He'll go to Brest and leave us to deal with the real murderer!'"

Maigret walked another twenty paces in silence. In the square, the market stalls were being dismantled.

"I almost told him that . . ."

"That what?"

Leroy blushed and turned his head away. "Exactly! I don't know . . . I, too, get the feeling that you don't think it's really important to catch the drifter."

"How's Mostaguen doing?"

"Better. He can't think of any reason he was attacked . . . He asked his wife's pardon, pardon for staying so late at the café. Pardon for being half drunk. He was in tears and swore he'd never touch another drop of alcohol."

Fifty yards from the Admiral Hotel, Maigret stopped to look at the harbor. Boats were coming in, dropping their brown sails as they rounded the breakwater, sculling slowly along.

At the base of the Old Town's walls, the ebb tide was uncovering banks of mud studded with old pots and other rubbish.

A faint suggestion of sun showed through the almost solid cloud cover.

"Your impression, Leroy?"

The inspector grew uneasy again. "I don't know . . . I think if we had that fellow . . . Remember that the yellow dog has disappeared again. What could the man have been up to in the doctor's house? There must have been some poisons there. I deduce from that—"

"Yes, of course. But I don't go in for deductions."

"Still, I'd be curious to see that drifter up close. From the footprints, he must be a giant—"

"Exactly."

"What do you mean?"

"Nothing."

Maigret lingered; he seemed delighted by the view of the little harbor: Cabélou Point to the left, with its pines and rocky headlands, the red-and-black tower, the scarlet buoys marking the channel out to the Glénan Islands, which were indistinguishable in the gray light.

The inspector still had a good deal to say. "I telephoned Paris to get information on Goyard; he lived there for a long time."

Maigret looked at him with affectionate irony, and, stung to the quick, Leroy recited briskly:

"The information is either very good or very bad. I got hold of a fellow who'd been a sergeant in the Vice Squad back then and had known him personally. It seems he moved for some time on the edges of journalism, first as a gossip columnist. Then he was manager of a little theater. Next he ran a cabaret in Montmartre. Went broke twice. For two years he was editor in chief of a provincial newspaper—at Nevers, I believe. Finally, he ran a night club. 'A fellow who knows how to stay afloat'—that's what the sergeant said . . . True, he also said, 'Not a bad guy. When he eventually saw that all he'd ever do was eat through his money or make trouble for himself, he decided to plunge back into small-town life.'"

"So?"

"So I wonder why he would fake that attack. I went back to look at the car. There *are* bloodstains, and they're real. If he was actually attacked, why wouldn't he have sent some message, since now he's walking around Brest?"

"Very good!"

The inspector looked sharply at Maigret to see if he was teasing. No. The superintendent was gazing seriously at a gleam of sunlight far out at sea.

"As for Le Pommeret—"

"You have a line on him?"

"His brother came to the hotel to speak to you. He couldn't stay. He had nothing but bad things to say about the dead man. As far as he was concerned, his brother was an absolute good-for-nothing. Interested only in women and hunting. And he had a mania for running up bills and for playing the lord of the manor . . . One detail out of the hundreds: the brother is probably the biggest manufacturer in the district, and he told me:

"'I'm satisfied to buy my clothes in Brest. Nothing fancy—just substantial, comfortable clothes. But Yves would go to Paris to order his clothes. And he had to have handmade shoes signed by a famous bootmaker! My own wife doesn't wear custom-made shoes.'"

"That's a joke!" said Maigret, to his companion's great bewilderment, if not indignation.

"Why?"

"All right, then, it's magnificent. To use your own expression, we're taking a real plunge into small-town life. And it's just like it's always been! Knowing whether Le Pommeret wore ready-made or custom-made shoes—that may not seem like much. But, believe it or not, that's the key to the story, right there . . . Let's go and get an aperitif, Leroy—like those fellows did every day at the Admiral café!"

Again the inspector looked at his chief to determine whether the man was making fun of him. He had been hoping for congratulations on his morning's work and for all his enterprise.

Instead, Maigret was behaving as though the whole thing were a joke!

————

The effect was the same as when the teacher enters a classroom where the students are chattering. Conversation stopped. The reporters rushed up to the superintendent.

"Can we report the doctor's arrest? Has he confessed?"

"Nothing at all!"

Maigret waved them aside and called to Emma, "Two Pernods, my dear."

"But look, if you've arrested Michoux—"

"You want to know the truth?"

They already had their notebooks in hand. They waited, pens at the ready.

"Well then, there is no truth yet. Maybe there will be some day. Maybe not."

"We hear that Jean Goyard—"

"Is alive. So much the better for him."

"But still, there's a man in hiding, and they can't find him."

"Which goes to prove the hunter's not as smart as the prey."

Taking Emma by the sleeve, Maigret said gently, "I'll have my lunch in my room."

He drank his aperitif down straight and got to his feet.

"A piece of advice, gentlemen! No jumping to conclusions. And no deductions, above all."

"What about the criminal?"

He shrugged his broad shoulders and murmured: "Who knows?"

He was already at the foot of the stairs. Inspector Leroy threw him a questioning look.

"No, my friend. You eat down here. I need a rest."

He climbed the stairs with heavy tread. Ten minutes later, Emma went up after him with a plate of hors d'oeuvres.

Then she carried up a *coquille St. Jacques* and roast veal with spinach.

In the dining room, conversation languished. One of the reporters was called to the phone.

"Around four o'clock, yes," he declared. "I hope to have something sensational for you . . . Not yet! We've got to wait . . ."

All alone at a table, Leroy ate with the manners of a well-bred boy, regularly wiping his lips with the corner of his napkin.

People outside kept an eye on the Admiral café, hoping vaguely for something to happen.

A policeman leaned against the building at the end of the alleyway where the vagrant had disappeared.

"The mayor is on the phone, asking for Superintendent Maigret," Emma announced.

Leroy jumped. "Go up and tell him," he said to her.

The waitress left, but came right back and said, "He's not there!"

The inspector bounded up the stairs four by four, returned very pale, and snatched the receiver.

"Hello! . . . Yes, *Monsieur le Maire* . . . I don't know. I . . . I'm worried. The superintendent is gone . . . No, that's all I can tell you. He had lunch in his room. I didn't see him come down . . . I . . . I'll phone you back."

Leroy, who had not put his napkin down, used it now to wipe his brow.

7

THE COUPLE BY CANDLELIGHT

Half an hour later, Leroy went up to his own room. On his table, he found a note in Morse code:

"Go up to the roof tonight at eleven. Let no one see you. I'll be there. No noise. Bring gun. Say that I left for Brest and phoned you from there. Don't leave hotel. Maigret."

A little before eleven, Leroy took off his shoes and put on some felt slippers he had bought that afternoon expressly for this expedition. He was somewhat apprehensive.

At the third floor, the staircase ended, but a fixed ladder led to a trap door in the ceiling. In the icy, drafty attic above, Leroy took the risk of lighting a match.

A few moments later, he climbed out through a skylight, but he didn't dare move down toward the eaves immediately. It was bitterly cold. His fingers froze on contact with the zinc shingles. And he had decided, unfortunately, not to saddle himself with an overcoat.

When his eyes adapted to the darkness, he seemed to make out a darker, stocky mass, like a huge animal lying in wait. He smelled pipe smoke, and whistled softly.

A moment later he was crouched on the ledge next to Maigret. Neither the sea nor the town was visible; they were on the slope of the roof away from the quay and over a black chasm that was the very alleyway through which the big-footed man had escaped.

Every perspective was out of line: there were some very low roofs and others at eye level. Some windows were lighted here and there. A few had blinds drawn, and a kind of Chinese shadow play moved across them. In a distant room, a woman was washing a baby in an enamel basin.

The superintendent's bulk moved, or, rather, shifted, over until his mouth was pressed to his companion's ear.

"Be careful! No sudden movements. The ledge isn't too solid, and right below us there's a gutter pipe waiting to drop off and make a racket. What about the reporters?"

"They're downstairs, except for one, who's gone to look for you in Brest. He's convinced you're on Goyard's trail."

"Emma?"

"I don't know. I wasn't keeping track of her . . . She did serve me coffee after dinner."

It was unsettling to be up here, unsuspected, on top of a house full of life—people moving around in warmth, in light, with no need to lower their voices.

"Now—turn carefully toward the house that's for sale . . . Careful!"

The house was the second to the right, one of the few as tall as the hotel. It was part of a block of total darkness, and yet the inspector made out what seemed to be a glint reflecting off a curtainless window on the third floor.

Little by little, he realized that it was not a reflection from outside, but a feeble light inside. He stared at that single point until things began to take shape. A shiny floor . . . a half-consumed candle, its flame burning straight up, ringed by a halo.

"He's there!" Leroy said suddenly, louder than he intended.

"Shh! Yes."

Someone was lying on the bare floor, half in candlelight, half in shadow. An enormous shoe, a broad torso molded by a sailor's sweater.

Leroy knew that there was a policeman at the end of the alley, another in the square, and still another patrolling the quay.

"Do you want to arrest him?"

"I don't know. He's been sleeping for three hours now."

"Is he armed?"

"He wasn't this morning."

The words were scarcely audible, more an indistinct murmur, almost like breathing.

"What are we waiting for?"

"I'm not sure. I'd like to know why he's kept a candle burning while he's asleep, especially when people are after him . . . Look!"

A yellow square appeared on a wall. "A light's gone on in Emma's room, right below us. That's the reflection."

"You had any dinner, superintendent?"

"I brought some bread and sausage . . . You're not cold?"

The two of them were frozen. They saw the glowing beam from the lighthouse sweep the sky at regular intervals.

"She's turned out the light."

"Yes. Shh!"

Five minutes of silence, a bleak wait. Then Leroy's hand reached for Maigret's, clasped it meaningfully. "Look down."

"I saw."

A shadow moved on the rough whitewashed wall that separated the garden of the vacant house from the alley.

"She's going to meet him," whispered Leroy, who could not keep silent.

Up above, the man was still asleep in the light of his candle. A currant bush swayed in the garden. A cat fled along a roof gutter.

"You wouldn't have a lighter with a long wick, would you?"

Maigret had not dared relight his pipe. After hesitating a long time, he finally screened himself with his companion's jacket and scratched a match sharply. The inspector soon smelled the warm odor of tobacco again.

"Look!"

They said nothing more. The man stood up so abruptly he nearly knocked the candle over. He drew back into the darkness as the door opened, and Emma appeared in the light, uncertain and so abject that she looked guilty.

From under her arm, she took a bottle and a package and set them on the floor. The paper, peeled back, showed a roast chicken.

She spoke. That is, her lips moved. She said only a few words, humbly, sadly. Her companion was out of sight of the two watchers.

Was she crying? She still had on her black waitress's dress and the Breton headdress. She had taken off only her white apron, and without it she looked even more woebegone.

Yes, she must have been crying as she said those few halting words. This was confirmed when she suddenly leaned against the door frame and buried her face in the crook of her arm. Her back shuddered fitfully.

The man suddenly appeared, blacking out nearly the whole square of the window, but he freed the view as he strode across the room. His great hand hit the girl's shoulder with such a jolt that she made a complete turn, nearly fell, and raised her poor pale face to him, her lips swollen with sobs.

But the scene was as indistinct, as hazy as a film when the house lights come up. And something was missing: sounds, voices . . . Like a film, a silent film without music.

Now the man was talking, apparently harshly. He was a bear. His head was hunched into his shoulders, and his sweater showed off his chest muscles. With his fists on his hips, he seemed to be shouting reproaches, or insults, perhaps even threats.

He looked so close to hitting the girl that Leroy drew closer to Maigret, as if for reassurance.

Emma was still weeping. Her headdress had slipped sideways. Her chignon was coming loose. A window slammed shut somewhere and brought a moment's distraction.

"Superintendent . . . shouldn't we . . ." Leroy began.

The scent of tobacco enveloped the two men and gave them an illusion of warmth.

Why was Emma clasping her hands? She was speaking again. Her face was distorted in an expression of fright, of pleading, of pain, and Leroy heard Maigret cock his revolver.

A mere fifteen or twenty yards separated the two pairs. A sharp report, a shattered windowpane, and the giant would be in no condition to do harm.

Now he was striding the length and breadth of the room, his hands behind his back. He seemed shorter, broader. His foot jostled the roast chicken. He nearly slipped, and furiously kicked it into the shadow.

Emma looked in that direction.

What could the two of them be saying? What was the subject of their heartbreaking dialogue?

The man seemed to be repeating the same words over again. But was it possible he was saying them more gently?

She fell to her knees, flung herself down in his path, and raised her arms toward him. He acted as if she were not there, evaded her grasp. Then she was no longer on her knees, but half sprawled, with one arm stretched out imploringly.

At one moment the man was visible; the next, the darkness swallowed him. When he reemerged, he stopped short before the pleading girl and looked down at her from on high.

Again he paced—came near, moved away—and she no

longer had the strength, or the heart, to reach out to him, to entreat. She slipped full length to the floor. The bottle of wine was inches from her hand.

Unexpectedly, the vagrant stooped, seized her dress at the shoulder in one of his huge paws, and, in one movement, set Emma on her feet. It was done so roughly that she swayed when she was no longer supported.

And yet, wasn't there some faint hope on her haggard face? Her hair was tumbled about. The white headdress trailed underfoot.

The man continued pacing. Twice, he strode past his distraught companion.

The third time, he took her in his arms, crushed her to him, tipped back her head, and greedily pressed his lips to hers.

All they could see was his back, a back not human, with a small female hand clamped on his shoulder.

Never taking his lips from hers, the creature stroked her straggling locks with his huge fingers, stroked as if he wanted to annihilate his companion, to crush her, to take her into himself.

"My God!" Leroy sounded overcome.

Maigret had been so moved that in reaction he nearly burst out laughing.

———

Had Emma been there a quarter of an hour? The embrace was over. The candle would last only another five minutes. And the atmosphere of relief was almost visible.

Was the waitress laughing? She had apparently found a mirror somewhere. They watched her, in the full light of the candle, roll up her long hair, fasten it with a pin, search the floor for another pin, and hold it between her teeth while she put the headdress back in place.

She was almost beautiful. She *was* beautiful! Everything about her was appealing, even her flat figure, her black dress, her red eyelids. The man had picked up the chicken and, without taking his eyes off her, was biting into it lustily, cracking the bones, tearing off strips of meat.

He felt, unsuccessfully, for a knife in his pocket, then snapped the neck of the bottle by knocking it against his heel. He drank. When he urged Emma to drink, she tried to refuse, laughing. Perhaps the jagged glass frightened her. But he made her open her mouth and gently poured in the liquid.

She choked and coughed. He took her by the shoulders and kissed her again, but this time not on the lips. He kissed her gleefully, giving little pecks on her cheeks, on her eyes, on her brow, and even on her lace headdress.

She was ready. He pressed his face to the window, and once again he almost totally filled the dim rectangle. When he turned away, it was to put out the candle.

Inspector Leroy stiffened. "They're leaving together . . ."

"Yes."

"They'll be caught . . ."

The currant bush in the garden trembled. A figure was hoisted to the top of the wall. Emma then stood in the alley waiting for her lover.

"Follow them, but keep your distance. Make sure they don't notice you! . . . Let me know what happens when you get a chance."

Just as the big man had done for his companion, Maigret helped the inspector hitch himself up the roof tiles to the skylight. Then he leaned over to look down into the alleyway, to see the tops of the fugitives' heads.

They hesitated, whispering. It was Emma who led the man toward a shed. They vanished into it, for the door was only latched.

It was a ship chandler's storage shed, connected to his shop, which would be empty at this hour. Just one lock to force, and the couple could reach the quay.

But Leroy would get there before them.

————

As he climbed down the attic ladder, the superintendent realized that something strange was happening. There was a commotion downstairs. And the telephone was ringing amid the clamoring voices.

Among them was Leroy's, louder than usual—he was apparently on the phone.

Maigret hurried down the stairs to the ground floor where he collided with one of the reporters.

"What's going on?" he asked.

"Another shooting . . . a quarter of an hour ago, in town . . . They took the victim to the pharmacy."

The superintendent darted out to the quay and saw a policeman running and brandishing his revolver. The sky was blacker than ever. Maigret caught up to the man and again asked, "What's going on?"

"A couple just came out of that store . . . I was on patrol across the way. The man practically fell into my arms . . . It's not worth chasing them now. They must be a long way off!"

"Explain what happened."

"I heard sounds in the shop, but there were no lights on. So I stood by with my gun ready. The door opened; a man came out . . . But I didn't even have time to take aim. He hit me in the face so hard that I fell down. I dropped my gun, and the one thing that scared me was that he'd grab it . . . But no—he went back to get a woman who was waiting in the doorway. She couldn't run, and he picked her up in his arms . . . By the time I got up, superintendent . . . That was some punch! Look, I'm bleeding! . . . They'd taken off along the quay. They must have gone around the harbor. And there are lots of little streets off there, and then it's all open country . . ."

The policeman was dabbing his nose with his handkerchief. "He could have killed me, just like that! He's got a fist like a sledgehammer."

Voices could still be heard in the hotel, which was all lit up. Maigret left the policeman, rounded the corner, and saw the pharmacy. Its shutters were closed, but its open door let out a flood of light.

Fifteen or twenty people were clustered at the door. The superintendent elbowed through them.

In the dispensary, a man laid out flat on the floor was emitting rhythmic moans as he stared at the ceiling.

The pharmacist's wife, in her nightgown, was making more noise than all the rest of them together.

And the pharmacist himself, who had slipped a jacket on over his pajamas, was in a panic, shuffling vials around, tearing open large packages of absorbent cotton.

"Who is it?" Maigret asked.

He didn't wait for the answer; he had already recognized the customs uniform, with the trouser leg slit open. And now he recognized the face.

It was the customs guard who had been on duty in the port the Friday before and had witnessed the Mostaguen shooting from a distance.

A doctor arrived in a rush, looked at the wounded man, then at Maigret, and cried, "What next?"

A little blood had run on to the floor. The pharmacist had washed the guard's leg with hydrogen peroxide, which left streaks of rosy foam.

Outside, a man was telling his tale, perhaps for the tenth time, but in a voice still gasping with excitement nonetheless:

"My wife and I were asleep when I heard a noise that sounded like a gunshot, and a cry! Then nothing more, for maybe five minutes. I didn't dare go back to sleep. My wife wanted me to go look. Then we heard these moans that sounded as if they were coming from right in front of our door. I opened it—I had a gun . . . and I saw a dark shape. I recognized the uniform. I shouted, to wake up the neighbors. And the fruit seller—he has a car—helped me bring the fellow here . . ."

"What time did you hear the shot?"

"Half an hour ago."

That was just when the scene was most intense between Emma and the man of the huge footprints.

"Where do you live?"

"I'm the sailmaker. You've passed my house a dozen times, on the right side of the harbor, past the fish market. My house is at the corner of the quay and a little street . . . After that, the buildings thin out, and there's almost nothing except private houses."

Four men carried the wounded customs guard into a back room, where they laid him on a couch. The doctor gave instructions. In the shop, the mayor's voice could be heard asking, "Is the superintendent here?"

Maigret went and stood in front of him, his hands in his pockets.

"You must admit, superintendent . . ."

But Maigret's look was so cold that the mayor was disconcerted for a moment.

"It's our man who did this . . . no?" he asked.

"No."

"How do you know?"

"I know because at the moment the crime was committed I had just as clear a view of him as I have of you right now."

"And you didn't arrest him?"

"No."

"I hear he assaulted a policeman, too."

"That's correct."

"Do you realize what repercussions this kind of thing could have? . . . You know, it's since you've been here that—"

Maigret picked up the telephone. "Give me the police barracks, mademoiselle—Yes, thanks . . . Hello! Is this the sergeant? Superintendent Maigret here. Dr. Michoux is still there, of course? . . . What's that? . . . Yes, go and check anyway. You've got a man posted in the court-yard? . . . Good. I'll wait."

"You think it's the doctor who—"

"Not at all! I never think anything, *Monsieur le Maire* . . . . Yes! He hasn't moved? Thank you . . . Asleep, eh? . . . Very good . . . No, nothing special."

Groans sounded from the back room, and soon a voice called, "Superintendent . . ."

It was the doctor, who was wiping his soapy hands on a towel. "You can question him now. The bullet only grazed his calf. He's more scared than hurt. Although I should say that he lost a lot of blood."

The customs man had tears in his eyes. He flushed when the doctor went on: "He was frightened because he thought we would cut off his leg . . . The fact is, in a week the thing won't even show."

The mayor stood framed in the doorway.

"Tell me how it happened," Maigret said gently as he sat on the edge of the couch. "Don't be afraid . . . You heard what the doctor said."

"I don't know . . ."

"Well, tell me what you can."

"I got off duty tonight at ten o'clock. I live a little past the corner where I was wounded—"

"You didn't go directly home?"

"No. The lights were still on at the Admiral. And I wanted to find out the latest . . . I swear my leg is burning up!"

"No, no, it's fine," the doctor said firmly.

"But I'm telling you . . . Well, as long as it's not serious. I had a beer at the café. Only the reporters were there, and I didn't have the nerve to ask them."

"Who served you?"

"A chambermaid, I think. I didn't see Emma."

"And then?"

"I headed for home. I stopped at the booth to light a cigarette off my colleague's pipe. Then I went along the quay, turned right . . . There was no one around. The sea was quite pretty . . . All of a sudden, just as I got a little past a corner, I felt a pain in my leg, even before I heard the shot. It felt like a cobblestone hitting me hard in the calf. I fell down . . . I tried to get up. Someone was running . . . Then my hand touched something hot and wet, and, I don't know how it happened, but I passed out . . . I thought I was dead . . .

"When I came to, the fruit seller at the corner had his

door open and was standing there, afraid to come out. That's all I know."

"You didn't see the person who fired?"

"I didn't see anything. It doesn't happen the way people think . . . There's a moment when you're falling down . . . and then when my hand felt the blood . . ."

"You don't have any enemies you can think of?"

"No. I've only been here two years . . . I come from inland . . . and in that time I've never spotted any smugglers."

"Do you always go home by that route?"

"No. That's the longest way . . . But I had no matches, and so I went over to the guardhouse to light my cigarette. Then, instead of cutting through town, I just went along the waterfront."

"It's shorter through town?"

"A little."

"So that someone who saw you leave the café and head along the quay would have had time to get in position for an ambush?"

"Oh, yes. But why? I never carry money on me . . . And anyhow, they didn't try to rob me."

"You're quite sure, superintendent, that you never lost sight of your drifter the whole evening?" There was an edge to the mayor's voice.

Leroy came in, holding out a piece of paper.

"A telegram. The post office has just phoned it to the hotel. It's from Paris."

And Maigret read:

Sûreté Générale to Superintendent Maigret, Concarneau. Jean Goyard, alias Servières, per your description, arrested Monday night at eight, Hotel Bellevue, Rue Lepic, Paris, while moving into room 15. Admits arriving from Brest by six o'clock train. Protests innocence and demands presence of counsel at further interrogation. Await instructions.

8

PLUS ONE

"You'll agree perhaps, superintendent, that it's time we had a serious talk . . ."

The mayor had said this in a tone of icy formality, and Inspector Leroy did not know Maigret well enough yet to judge his reaction from the way he blew out his pipe smoke. A slender gray stream emerged slowly from the superintendent's half-open lips, and he blinked two or three times. Then he drew his notebook from his pocket and looked around at the pharmacist, the doctor, the bystanders.

"At your service, *Monsieur le Maire* . . . Here is—"

"If you'd like to have a cup of tea at my house," the mayor interrupted hastily, "I have my car at the door. I'll wait till you've given the necessary orders."

"What orders?"

"But . . . the murderer, the drifter . . . that girl . . . ?"

"Oh, yes! Well, if the police have nothing better to do, they can keep an eye on the railway stations round here." He wore his most ingenuous expression. "Leroy, wire Paris to send Goyard here. Then go to bed."

He got in the mayor's car, which was driven by a

chauffeur in black livery. As they neared White Sands, they caught sight of the mayor's house. It was built directly on the cliff, which made it look somewhat like a feudal château. Lights shone from several windows.

The two men had barely exchanged two sentences in the course of the drive. "Allow me to show you a few points of interest," the mayor had tried.

At the villa, he handed his fur coat to a butler. "Madame has gone to bed?"

"No, sir. She is waiting for you in the library."

They found her there. She was about forty years old and looked young next to her husband, who was sixty-five. She nodded to the superintendent.

"Well?"

Very much the man of the world, the mayor kissed her hand, which he kept in his as he said, "Don't worry. A customs guard was slightly wounded . . . And I hope that after the conversation we're about to have, Superintendent Maigret and I, this unconscionable nightmare will come to an end."

She left, with a rustle of silk. A blue plush drape fell back into place at the door.

The huge library had walls lined with fine paneling and exposed ceiling beams, like those in an English manor house. Fairly rich bindings could be seen on the shelves, but more precious ones were apparently kept in a closed bookcase that covered one whole wall.

The setting was one of real luxury, faultless taste, utter

comfort. There was central heating, but logs blazed in a monumental fireplace. There was no comparison with the false elegance of the doctor's house.

The mayor selected a box of cigars and held it out to Maigret.

"Thank you! If you'll allow me, I'll smoke my pipe."

"Please sit down . . . Will you have a whiskey?"

He pressed a buzzer, then lit a cigar. The butler came in to serve them. And, perhaps on purpose, Maigret seemed to have the awkward manner of a petit bourgeois visiting an aristocratic house. His features looked heavy, his gaze vague.

His host waited for the butler to leave. "I'm sure you understand, superintendent, that this series of crimes cannot go on. It's been . . . let's see . . . three days now since you arrived. And in all that time—"

From his pocket Maigret drew his cheap little oilcloth-covered notebook.

"May I?" he interrupted. "You mention a series of crimes . . . Now I'd like to point out that all the victims are alive except one. A single death: Monsieur Le Pommeret's . . . As for the customs guard, you'll admit that anyone who really wanted to kill him would not have shot him in the leg. You know where the shot was fired from. The attacker was hidden, so he could take all the time he needed. Unless he'd never held a revolver before . . ."

The mayor looked at him with astonishment, and, seizing his glass, said, "So you claim—"

"That the assailant meant to wound him in the leg . . . At least until we have proof to the contrary."

"Did Monsieur Mostaguen's assailant mean to hit him in the leg, too?"

The sarcasm was obvious, and the man's nostrils quivered. He was straining to be polite, to keep calm, because he was in his own home. But there was a disagreeable edge to his voice.

His manner that of a proper civil servant reporting to his superior, Maigret went on:

"If you'll allow me, we'll go over my notes one by one . . . . I read from the date of Friday, November 7: *A bullet is fired through the letter box of a vacant house toward Monsieur Mostaguen.* Remember, to begin with, that no one, not even the victim, could have known that at a given moment Monsieur Mostaguen would get the idea of stopping in a doorway to light his cigar. A little less wind and the crime would never have occurred . . . Of course, there *was* a man with a revolver behind the door . . . . Either he was crazy or he was waiting for *someone who was supposed to come.* Now then, remember what time it was. Eleven o'clock at night. The whole town was asleep, except for the little group at the Admiral café.

"I'm drawing no conclusions, but let's run through the possible guilty parties. Le Pommeret and Jean Servières, and Emma too, are out of the running, because they were still in the café.

"That leaves Dr. Michoux, who had left fifteen minutes

earlier, and the vagrant with the enormous footprints. Plus an unknown person we'll call X. Are we in agreement? . . .

"We should add, parenthetically, that Monsieur Mostaguen did not die and that in two weeks he'll be on his feet again . . .

"Let's go to the second incident. *The following day, Saturday, I enter the café. After introductions, I am about to drink an aperitif with Messieurs Michoux, Le Pommeret, and Jean Servières when the doctor suddenly becomes suspicious of something in his glass. Analysis shows the Pernod bottle to be poisoned.*

"Possible culprits: Michoux, Le Pommeret, Servières; Emma, the waitress; the vagrant—who might have entered the café sometime during the day without being seen—and also our unknown person designated X.

"Let's continue. *Sunday morning, Jean Servières disappears. His car is found, with bloodstains, not far from his home. Before this discovery, the* Brest Beacon *receives a report of the events nicely calculated to sow panic in Concarneau.*

"*Then Servières is seen, first in Brest, later in Paris, where he seems to be hiding and to which he has apparently gone of his own free will.*

"Only one possible culprit here: Servières himself.

"*The same day, Sunday, Monsier Le Pommeret has an aperitif with the doctor, returns to his home, has dinner there, and dies afterward, from the effects of strychnine poisoning.*

"Possible culprits: at the café, if that's where he was poisoned, the doctor, Emma, and again our X. This time, the vagrant has to be ruled out, because the café was never empty for a moment, and it wasn't the bottle that was poisoned—only the one glass.

"If the crime was committed in Le Pommeret's own house, possible culprits: his landlady, the vagrant, and our sempiternal X.

"Bear with me now; we're coming to the end. *Tonight, Monday, a customs guard is shot in the leg as he walks down an empty street. The doctor is still in prison, under close watch. Le Pommeret is dead. Servières is in Paris in the hands of the Sûreté. Emma and the vagrant are at that very moment embracing and then devouring a chicken, before my own eyes.*

"Thus, only one possible culprit: X. That is to say, a person we haven't yet encountered in the course of events. A person who could have committed all the crimes, or only this last one.

"We don't know who this person is. We have no description of him. Just one clue: whoever it is, he was interested in making something happen tonight—had a pressing interest. That bullet wasn't fired by a random prowler.

"Now, don't ask me to arrest X. Because you'll agree, *Monsieur le Maire,* that anyone in town—especially someone who knows the principal characters involved in this business and, in particular, the regular customers at the Admiral café—could be that X.

"Even you."

These last words were spoken casually as Maigret leaned back in his chair and stretched his legs toward the fire. The mayor gave the merest start. "I hope that's just a little retaliation . . ."

Then Maigret stood up suddenly, knocked out his pipe on the hearth, and declared, as he walked up and down:

"Not at all! You wanted answers? Well, there you are. I just wanted to show you that a case like this is no simple little police operation that can be handled by making a few telephone calls from an armchair . . . And I will add, *Monsieur le Maire,* with all due respect, that when I take charge of an investigation, I insist above all, damn it, on being *left alone!*"

That came out with no premeditation. It had been incubating for days. Perhaps to calm down, Maigret took a swallow of whiskey and looked at the door like a man who has said what he has to say and is waiting for permission to leave.

The mayor was silent for a few minutes, contemplating the white ash of his cigar. Finally, he let it fall into a blue porcelain bowl and rose slowly, his eyes seeking Maigret's.

"Listen, superintendent . . ."

He must have been weighing his words, for they were separated by pauses.

"I may have been wrong, in the course of our brief connection, to show some impatience . . ."

This was rather unexpected—especially in this setting, where the man seemed more aristocratic than ever, with his white hair, his silk-trimmed smoking jacket, his sharply creased gray trousers.

"I am beginning to appreciate your true worth. In these few minutes, by means of a simple summary of the facts, you've made me understand the terrible mystery of this business. It's more complex than I ever suspected. I confess your inertia in the matter of the vagrant did dispose me against you." He approached the superintendent and touched his shoulder. "I ask you not to hold it against me . . . I have some heavy responsibilities myself."

It would have been impossible to guess Maigret's thoughts as his thick fingers packed his pipe from a worn tobacco pouch. Through a large window, his gaze wandered over the vast ocean horizon.

"What's that light?" he asked suddenly.

"The beacon."

"No, I mean that small light to the right."

"That's Dr. Michoux's house."

"The servant's back, then?"

"No. It's Madame Michoux, the doctor's mother. She came back this afternoon."

"You've seen her?"

Maigret thought he sensed some discomfort in his host.

"Well, she was surprised not to find her son at home. She came by to ask. I told her about the arrest, explaining that it was mainly a protective measure . . . Because that's what it is, isn't it? She asked my authorization to visit him . . . At the hotel, no one knew where you were. So I took it on myself to permit the visit.

"Madame Michoux came back shortly before dinner to ask for the latest news. My wife invited her to eat with us."

"They're friends?"

"In a manner of speaking. Good neighbors is more accurate. In the winter, there are very few people in Concarneau."

Maigret resumed his stroll across the library. "So the three of you ate together?"

"Yes. That often happens . . . I reassured Madame Michoux as best I could. She was quite upset by the business of the police barracks . . . She had a difficult time raising her son; his health has never been very good."

"Did you discuss Le Pommeret and Jean Servières?"

"She never liked Le Pommeret. She claimed he led her son to drink. The fact is that—"

"And Servières?"

"She didn't know him as well. He didn't move in her circle. An unimportant newspaperman, a café acquaintance— merely an amusing fellow. One couldn't, for example, receive his wife, a woman whose past is not entirely above reproach . . . That's small-town life, superintendent! You've got to resign yourself to these distinctions. They partly explain my own short temper. You don't know what it is to manage a community of fishermen and at the same time watch out for the sensibilities of the gentry—and of some middle-class elements besides—"

"What time did Madame Michoux leave here?"

"About ten. My wife drove her back in the car."

"That light means that Madame Michoux hasn't gone to bed yet."

"That's usual for her . . . For me as well. At a certain age, we need less sleep. Very late at night I'm still in here reading, or looking over files—"

"Are the Michouxs doing well with their business?"

Uneasiness showed again, though barely perceptible.

"Not yet . . . It will take time for the White Sands project to begin producing a profit. But, given Madame Michoux's connections in Paris, that shouldn't be long. A number of plots have been sold already, and construction will start again in the spring. On this recent trip, she practically persuaded a certain banker whose name I can't mention to build a magnificent house on the bluff . . ."

"One more question, *Monsieur le Maire*: who used to own the land they're developing?"

His companion did not hesitate. "I did. It belonged to my family, as did this house. There was nothing there but heather and broom when the Michouxs got the idea—"

Just then the distant light went out.

"Another whiskey, superintendent? . . . Of course, I'll have my chauffeur drive you back."

"You're very kind. But I love to walk, especially when I have things to think over."

"What do you make of this business of the yellow dog? I confess that that may be what upsets me most—that and the poisoned Pernod! Because actually—"

But Maigret was looking around for his hat and coat.

The mayor had no choice but to press the buzzer. "The superintendent's things, Delphin."

The silence was so complete that they could hear the muffled, rhythmic sound of the surf on the rocks below the villa.

"You're sure you don't want my car?"

"Quite sure."

Wisps of discomfiture hung in the air like the wisps of tobacco smoke coiling about the lamps.

"I wonder what the mood will be in town tomorrow. If the sea is calm, at least we won't have the fishermen on the streets. They'll leap at the chance to set out their lobster pots."

Maigret took his coat from the butler and put out his big hand. The mayor still had questions, but he was reluctant to ask them in the butler's presence.

"How much longer do you think—"

The clock struck one in the morning.

"I hope it will all be cleared up by tomorrow night."

"So soon? Despite what you told me earlier? Then you must be counting on Goyard? . . . Unless—"

He was too late. Maigret had started down the stairs. The mayor searched for some last words, but nothing came to mind that expressed his feeling. "I'm uncomfortable letting you go back on foot—along those roads—"

The door closed. Maigret was on his way, under a fine sky with heavy clouds that raced one another across the moon. The air was sharp. The wind, from off the water, brought the smell of the seaweed strewn in dark masses on the beach.

The superintendent walked slowly, his hands in his pockets, his pipe between his teeth. Looking back, he saw the lights go out in the mayor's library, then others going on behind upstairs curtains.

He did not take the road through town, but followed the shore, as the customs guard had, and stopped for a moment at the corner where the man had been shot. All was calm. Streetlamps shone here and there into the distance. Concarneau was asleep.

When he reached the square, he saw that the café windows were still shining, violating the nocturnal peace with their poisonous halo. He pushed the door open. A reporter was dictating over the phone:

". . . By now no one knows whom to suspect. In the streets, people look anxiously at one another. Could this be the killer? Or maybe that one over there? The cloud of mystery and fear has never been so thick . . ."

The innkeeper himself stood gloomily at the till. The moment he caught sight of the superintendent, he made a move to approach and speak. It was easy enough to guess his complaints.

The café was a shambles, with newspapers and empty glasses on the tables. A photographer was busy drying prints on the radiator.

Inspector Leroy walked over to his chief. "That's Madame Goyard," he said in an undertone, pointing to a plump woman collapsed on a banquette.

She rose, wiping her eyes.

"Tell me, superintendent, is it true? . . . I don't know who to believe any more. They say Jean is alive. But it's impossible—isn't it?—that he would trick us like that. He wouldn't have done that to me. He would never put me through such worry . . . I feel as though I'm going mad!— Why would he have gone to Paris? Tell me! . . . And without me!"

She wept—the way certain women can weep, with great floods of tears pouring down her cheeks, flowing to her chin, while one hand pressed against her plump bosom. She looked for her handkerchief.

"I swear it can't be true!" she insisted. "I know he ran around a little . . . but he would never do anything like this. Whenever he came home, he asked me to forgive him . . . They're saying"—she pointed to the reporters— "they're saying he put the bloodstains in the car himself, to make it look like murder. But that would mean he never meant to come back! And I know better. I'm sure he would have . . . He never would have gone gallivanting if the others hadn't dragged him along—Monsieur Le Pommeret, the doctor . . . and the mayor too! That whole bunch, who never even greet me in the street, because I'm not good enough for them . . .

"Someone said he's been arrested . . . I don't believe it. What harm did he ever do? He earned enough for the kind of life we led. We were happy, even if he did treat himself to a fling once in while . . ."

Maigret looked at her and sighed. Then he picked up a

glass from a table, swallowed the contents straight down, and murmured, "You'll have to excuse me, madame. I've got to get some sleep."

"Do you believe it too—that he's done something wrong?"

"I never believe anything. You should do the same, madame. Tomorrow is another day."

And as he climbed the stairs heavily, the reporter at the phone turned Maigret's parting words to his own account:

"According to the latest word, Superintendent Maigret expects to clear up the mystery by tomorrow."

His tone changed as he finished. "That's all, mademoiselle. Now be sure to tell the boss not to change one line of my story. He couldn't understand . . . he'd have to be on the scene . . ."

Hanging up, he shoved his notes into his pocket and called to the proprietor, "Give me a toddy! Lots of rum and just a splash of hot water."

Meanwhile, Madame Goyard accepted a reporter's offer to drive her back to her house. On the way she began again: "He did run around a little . . . but you know how it is, monsieur! All men do that!"

9

THE SEASHELL BOX

Maigret was in such good spirits in the morning that Inspector Leroy felt free to follow him around, chattering and even asking some questions.

In fact, everyone was more relaxed, though it would be hard to say why. It may have been the weather, which had suddenly turned fine. The sky looked freshly laundered. It was blue, a rather pale but vibrant blue, glistening with light clouds. It made the horizon bigger, as if the celestial bowl were hollowed out. The sea sparkled, utterly flat and studded with tiny sails that looked like flags pinned to a military map.

It takes but a single sunbeam to transform Concarneau. Then the Old Town's walls, so gloomy in the rain, turn a joyful, dazzling white.

Exhausted by the comings and goings of the past three days, the reporters sat downstairs telling each other stories over coffee; one of them had come down in his dressing gown and slippers.

Meanwhile, Maigret had gone into Emma's attic room. The slope of the roof allowed standing up straight in only half the space. The gable window, which looked over the alleyway, was open. The air was cool, but it had the caressing feel of the sun in it. Across the way, a woman had taken the opportunity to hang her laundry out of her window. The noise of children came up from a school playground somewhere nearby.

Leroy, sitting on the edge of the little iron bed, remarked, "I still don't quite understand your methods, superintendent, but I think I'm beginning to see . . ."

Maigret gave him an amused glance and sent a large cloud of smoke out into the sunshine. "You're lucky, my friend! Especially in this case, in which my method has actually been not to have one . . . I'll give you some good advice: if you're interested in getting ahead, don't take me for a model, or invent any theories from what you see me doing."

"Still . . . I do notice that you're getting round to hard evidence now, after—"

"Exactly—after! After everything else! In other words, I ran this investigation from the end, backward—which doesn't mean I won't go the other way in the next one. It's a question of atmosphere, a question of faces . . . When I first got here, I came across one face that appealed to me, and I never let go of it."

But he did not say whose face he meant. He lifted aside an old sheet that hid a wardrobe. Inside hung a black velvet Breton costume, which Emma probably saved for special occasions.

On the dressing table were a comb with several teeth

missing, some hairpins, and a box of too-pink face powder.
In a drawer he found what he seemed to be looking for: a
box encrusted with shiny seashells, the kind sold in souvenir shops all along the coast. This one, which looked
perhaps ten years old and as though it had weathered God
knows what travels, bore the words *Souvenir of Ostend*.

The smell of old cardboard, dust, perfume, and yel-
lowed paper rose from it. Maigret sat down on the edge of
the bed beside his companion and, with his large fingers,
lifted out the inventory of tiny items.

There was a rosary of faceted blue glass beads on a
flimsy silver chain, a first communion medal, and an
empty perfume bottle that Emma must have found abandoned in a guest's room and saved for its appealing
shape . . .

A paper flower, the keepsake from some dance or festi-
val, struck a lively red note. Beside it was a small gold cru-
cifix, the only object of any value . . .

A whole pile of postcards . . . One showed a large hotel
in Cannes. On the back, in a woman's handwriting:

You reely awt to come here, insted of sticking in
that awful hole were it rains all the time. And we
earn good mony here. We get all we want to eat.
Big kiss—Louise.

Maigret passed the card to Leroy and stared attentively
at one of those photographs that are won at a fair by hitting the bull's-eye. Because of the rifle on his shoulder,

they could barely see the man taking aim, with one eye shut. He had an enormous build, and a sailor's cap on his head. Emma, grinning into the lens, gripped his arm proudly. At the bottom of the card was the name *Quimper.*

Next was a letter, on paper so tattered that it must have been reread many times:

> Darling,
>
> It's done, it's signed: I have my boat. She'll be called the *Pretty Emma.* The Quimper priest promised he would christen her next week, with holy water, grains of wheat, salt and all, and there will be real champagne, because I want it to be a party people will talk about for a long time around here.
>
> It will be hard to pay for her at first, because I have to hand the bank 10,000 francs a year. But just think, she'll carry over 3,000 square feet of sail and make ten knots. There's good money in carrying onions to England. What I mean is that it won't be too long before we can get married. I've already found a cargo for the first trip but they're trying to bargain me down, because I'm new.
>
> Your boss ought to give you two days off for the christening because everyone will be drunk and you won't be able to get back to Concarneau. I've had to treat everyone in the cafés round here to celebrate the boat, which is already in port and flying a brand-new flag.

I'll get my picture taken on board and send you
one. I kiss you with all my heart, waiting for the
day when you'll be the beloved wife of your
Léon.

Gazing dreamily at the drying laundry on the other side
of the alley, Maigret slipped the letter into his pocket.
There was nothing else in the shell box but a pen holder
carved of bone; a little glass lens in the base showed a view
of the crypt at Notre-Dame de Lourdes.

"Is there anyone in the room the doctor generally uses?"
he asked.

"I don't think so. The reporters are on the third floor."

Out of duty, the superintendent searched the room
again, but he found nothing else of interest. A little later,
down on the second floor, he opened the door to Michoux's
room, the one with the balcony overlooking the port and
the roadstead.

The bed was made, the floor polished. There were
clean towels on the washstand.

The inspector watched his chief with a mixture of curiosity and scepticism. But Maigret whistled a quiet tune
as he looked around, then headed for a small oak table in
front of the window. On it lay a promotional writing folder
and an ashtray.

Inside the folder were white paper with the hotel's let-
terhead and a blue envelope to match. But there were also
two large sheets of blotting paper—one nearly black with
ink, the other barely marked with sketchy characters.

"Go and get a mirror, son!"

"A big one?"

"Doesn't matter. Just one I can set up on the table."

When the inspector returned, he found Maigret planted on the balcony, his thumbs hooked in the armholes of his waistcoat, smoking his pipe with obvious satisfaction.

"Will this do?"

The balcony window was closed again. Maigret stood the mirror on the table and, using two candlesticks from the mantel, he set the sheet of blotting paper upright in front of it.

The characters reflected in the mirror were far from easy to read. Letters, even whole words, were missing. Others were so distorted that he could only guess at them.

"I see what you're after!" said Leroy, looking sly.

"Good! Now go ask the proprietor for one of Emma's account books, or anything else with her handwriting on it."

With a pencil he transcribed words on a sheet of paper: ". . . see you . . . o'clock . . . vacant . . . absolutely . . ."

By the time the inspector returned, Maigret had filled in the blanks roughly and pieced together the following note:

I need to see you. Come tomorrow night at eleven
to the vacant house on the square, a few doors past
the hotel. I'm absolutely counting on you. Just
knock and I'll open the door.

"Here's the book Emma keeps for the laundry," Leroy announced.

"It's the same writing. And look—the letter is signed. An initial E . . . And the letter was written here in this room."

"Where she spent nights with the doctor?" The inspector was aghast.

Maigret could understand his repugnance at accepting this idea, especially after the scene they had witnessed the night before from their perch on the roof.

"In that case, then she's the one who—"

"Easy! Easy, my boy! No jumping to conclusions. And no deductions, remember? . . . What time does Jean Goyard's train get in?"

"Eleven thirty-two."

"Here's what you're going to do, my friend. First, tell our two colleagues with him to bring the fellow to me at the police barracks . . . He'll get there at about noon. Telephone the mayor that I'd like to see him at the same time, same place . . . Wait! Same message for Madame Michoux—phone her at home . . . Then, at some point, the local police or others will probably be bringing in Emma and her sweetheart. Same place, same time for them . . . Am I forgetting anyone? . . . Good! Just one thing: Emma's not to be questioned in my absence. In fact, stop her from talking if she tries."

"The customs guard?"

"I don't need him."

"Monsieur Mostaguen?"

"Hmm . . . no. That's all."

In the café, Maigret ordered the local brandy and

sipped it with visible pleasure as he remarked to the news-papermen:

"We're winding up, gentlemen. You should be getting back to Paris tonight."

————

His walk through the Old Town's twisting streets added to his good humor. And when he reached the gateway to the police barracks, with the bright French flag above it, he noticed that, by some magical effect of the sunlight, the three colors, and the wall rippling with light, there was a kind of Bastille Day gaiety to the atmosphere.

An elderly policeman was sitting inside the gate reading a humorous magazine. The courtyard, with its small paving stones marked off by strips of green moss, was still as serene as a cloister.

"The sergeant?"

"They're all out—the lieutenant, the sergeant, and most of the men—looking for that drifter."

"The doctor hasn't budged?"

The man smiled and looked at a barred prison window to the right. "No danger of that."

"Open the door for me, will you?"

As soon as the bolts were drawn, Maigret exclaimed, in a bright, cordial voice: "Hello there, doctor! Slept well, I hope!"

But all he saw was a pale, knife-sharp face emerging from the gray blanket on the bunk. The eyes were feverish, sunk deep into their sockets.

"Well now, what's the trouble? Something wrong?"

"Very wrong," mumbled Michoux, raising himself with a sigh. "My kidney . . ."

"They're giving you whatever you need, I hope?"

"Yes . . . Good of you . . ."

He had gone to bed fully dressed, which was apparent when he slid his legs from under the blanket. He sat up and wiped his hand over his forehead.

Meanwhile, Maigret, bursting with health and vigor, straddled a chair and planted his elbows on its back.

"Well now! I see you ordered yourself a nice bottle of Burgundy!"

"My mother brought it yesterday . . . I would just as soon have skipped that visit. She must have got wind of something in Paris . . . She came back."

The dark circles under his eyes seemed to cover half of his unshaven hollow cheeks. The lack of a tie and his crumpled suit added to his aura of distress.

He cleared his throat and spat conspicuously into his handkerchief, which he then examined like a man worried about tuberculosis and keeping an anxious watch on himself.

"Is there anything new?" he asked warily.

"The police must have told you about last night."

"No! What hap . . . Who's been . . . ?" He cowered against the wall as if afraid of being attacked.

"Nothing serious. Someone was shot in the leg."

"Did they get the . . . whoever did it? . . . I can't take any more, superintendent! You have to admit it's enough to drive a person crazy . . . Someone else from the Admiral café. Am I right? We're the ones he's after! And I'm racking my brain to work out why . . . Yes, why? Mostaguen! Le Pommeret! And the poison—that was meant for all of us together . . . You'll see, they'll get me, no matter what, even in here! . . . But why? Tell me!"

He was no longer just pale. He was livid. It was painful to see such a picture of panic at its most pathetic and repellent.

"I don't even dare fall asleep . . . That window—look! There are bars, yes, but someone could shoot between them, at night. Suppose a guard fell asleep, or let his mind wander . . . I'm not made for this kind of life. Yesterday I drank that whole bottle, in hopes of getting to sleep, but I never closed an eye. I just felt sick. If they'd only kill that drifter, with his yellow dog . . . Did he turn up again, the dog? Is he still prowling around the café? . . . I don't understand why nobody's put a bullet into his hide. His and his master's both!"

"His master left Concarneau last night."

"Oh!" The doctor seemed to have some trouble believing that. "Right after—after his latest attack?"

"Before."

"But—that's impossible! That would mean—"

"Correct. That's what I was telling the mayor, last night . . . Odd character, the mayor. Just between you and me, what do you think of him?"

"Me? I don't know . . . I . . ."

"Well, he sold you the land for the development. You're involved with him. You were friends, so to speak."

"Our relations were mainly on business and as neighbors . . . out here in the country, you know . . ."

Maigret noticed that the doctor's voice was growing firmer, his glance less distracted.

"What was it you were telling him?" Michoux asked.

Maigret pulled his notebook from his pocket. "I was saying that the series of crimes—or murder attempts, if you like—couldn't have been committed by any of the persons now known to us. I won't go over the events one by one; I'll just summarize. I speak objectively, you understand, as a technician . . . Well, obviously you were in no position last night to fire at the customs guard, which could be enough to rule you out altogether. Le Pommeret couldn't have shot him either, since they're burying him tomorrow morning. Neither could Goyard; he's just been found in Paris . . . And they couldn't, any of them, have been the person behind the letter box in the vacant house last Friday . . . . Nor could Emma."

"What about the drifter with the yellow dog?"

"I considered him. Not only is he probably not the one who poisoned Le Pommeret, but last night he was a long way from where the shooting occurred . . . That's why I told the mayor that it might be some unknown person, some mysterious X, who committed all these crimes. Unless . . ."

"Unless?"

"Unless it's not one person. Instead of some sort of uni-lateral offensive, suppose there's actually a battle going on between two groups, or between two individuals."

"But what happens to me then, superintendent? If there are unknown enemies prowling around, I . . ." And his face went dull again. He put his head in his hands. "When I think how sick I am, and how the doctors tell me I need absolute calm! . . . Oh, there's no need for any bullet or poison to do me in. You'll see—my kidney will take care of that."

"What do you think of the mayor?"

"I don't know! I don't know anything about him! . . . He comes from a very rich family. When he was young, he lived the high life in Paris, had his own racing stable. And then he straightened out. He took the rest of his money and came to settle here, in the house built by his grandfather, who used to be mayor of Concarneau himself . . . He sold me the land he didn't need. I think he'd like to be appointed to the district council, and then move on to the Senate."

The doctor had stood up, and anyone would have sworn he had lost fifteen pounds in the last few days. It would have been no surprise, moreover, to see him burst into nervous tears.

"What do you think is going on? . . . What about Goyard, turning up in Paris when everyone thinks . . . What could he have been doing there? And why?"

"We'll soon find out, because he's about to arrive in Concarneau. In fact, he should be here by now."

"Is he under arrest?"

"He was asked to come along with two gentlemen. That's not the same thing."

"What did he say?"

"Nothing. But then, no one asked him anything."

The doctor suddenly looked the superintendent square in the face. A quick flush rose to his cheeks.

"What does that mean? . . . I get the impression that something crazy is going on. You come in here and chat about the mayor, about Goyard . . . and meanwhile I'm sure—you hear me?—I'm convinced, more and more, that I'm about to be killed! In spite of those bars. Never mind that big idiot policeman on duty out in the courtyard! . . . And I don't want to die! I don't! Just give me a revolver to defend myself. Or else lock up the people who are after me, the ones who killed Le Pommeret, who put poison in the bottle . . ."

He was panting. "I'm no hero! Facing death isn't my job. I'm just a man. A sick man! And I've got enough to do just fighting this disease . . . You talk and you talk, but what exactly are you doing?"

In a rage, he knocked his forehead against the wall. "This whole thing looks like a conspiracy to me . . . unless people are trying to drive me crazy! That's it—they want to commit me! . . . Who knows? Maybe it's my mother. She's probably had enough of me. Because I've always hung on to my share of my father's legacy. But I won't let them get away with this!"

Maigret had not moved. He sat there quietly—his elbows on the back of the chair, his pipe in his teeth—in the middle of the white cell with one wall drenched in sunlight.

The doctor moved back and forth, his agitation close to delirium.

Then suddenly there was the sound of a cheerful voice, a touch ironic, imitating a child's. "Coocoo!"

Ernest Michoux jumped and looked into all four corners of the cell before he turned to stare hard at Maigret. The superintendent had taken his pipe from his mouth and was looking at Michoux with a wide grin.

It was as if a switch had been flipped. Michoux stopped short, went limp. His substance seemed to fade to a ghostly mist.

"Was that you?" he asked.

The voice might have come from anywhere, like a ventriloquist's, springing from the ceiling or out of a china vase.

Maigret's eyes were still laughing as he rose and, in a tone entirely at odds with his expression, said: "Pull yourself together, doctor! I hear footsteps in the courtyard. In a few moments, I expect the murderer to be right here within these four walls."

It was the mayor the guard brought in first. But there were sounds of others in the courtyard.

10

THE *PRETTY EMMA*

"You asked me to come, superintendent?"

Before Maigret had time to answer, he saw two inspectors enter the courtyard with Jean Goyard between them; out in the street, an excited crowd had gathered around the gate.

The journalist looked smaller, plumper, between his two bodyguards. He had pulled his soft hat down over his eyes, and, probably worried about photographers, held a handkerchief over the lower part of his face.

"This way!" Maigret told the policemen. "You might get us some chairs, since I hear a female voice."

"Where is he?" a shrill voice demanded. "I want to see him immediately! And I'll have you demoted, young fellow—you hear me? I'll have you demoted . . ."

It was Madame Michoux, in a mauve dress and wearing her jewels, powder and rouge, and seething with anger.

"Ah! You're here, dear friend," she simpered, addressing the mayor. "Can you imagine such a thing? This little man arrives at my house before I'm even dressed—my maid is away—and I tell him, through the door, that I cannot receive him. He insists, he demands, he waits while I get ready, claiming he has an order to bring me here. It's simply outrageous! When I think that my husband was a deputy, practically prime minister, and that this . . . this lout—yes, lout . . ."

She was too indignant to register what was going on around her. Suddenly, she saw Goyard, averting his head, and her son sitting on the edge of his bunk with his head in his hands.

A car drove into the sunny courtyard at that point. Police uniforms gleamed. And a clamor rose from the crowd.

A guard had closed the gate, to keep the throng from forcing its way into the courtyard. For the first person to be pulled out of the car, literally, was none other than the drifter. Not only did he have handcuffs on his wrists, but his ankles were shackled with sturdy rope and he had to be dragged in like a sack.

Behind him came Emma, her limbs free but her movements dazed, as though she were in a dream.

"Untie his legs!" Maigret commanded.

The police were proud and elated over their catch. It couldn't have been an easy one, to judge by their disheveled uniforms and, especially, by the prisoner's face, which was smeared with the blood still running from his split lip.

Madame Michoux gave a frightened cry and recoiled against the wall. The man let himself be freed without a word, lifted his head, and gazed slowly around.

"Easy there, eh, Léon?" growled Maigret.

The man started, and looked around again, to see who had spoken.

"Someone give him a chair and a handkerchief."

Maigret noticed that Goyard had sidled to the farthest reach of the cell, behind Madame Michoux, and that the doctor was trembling and looking at no one. The police lieutenant was wondering uncomfortably what his role should be in this unusual assembly.

"Please close the door. Will everyone kindly be seated . . . Lieutenant, can your sergeant take down the proceedings? . . . Very good! He can sit at that little table. I'll ask you to have a seat too, *Monsieur le Maire.*"

The crowd outside was no longer shouting, but it was unmistakably present—a kind of dense vitality, of passionate attention out in the street.

Maigret stuffed his pipe as he paced the cell. Turning to Inspector Leroy, he said: "Before we start, I'd like you to telephone the seamen's association at Quimper to ask what happened, four or five years ago—maybe six—to a boat called the *Pretty Emma.*"

As Leroy headed for the door, the mayor coughed and indicated that he had something to say.

"I can tell you about that, superintendent. Everyone knows the story around here."

"Go on."

The vagrant tensed in his corner like an attack dog. Emma, sitting on the very edge of her chair, never took her eyes off him. Chance had put her beside Madame Michoux, whose perfume, a sugary violet scent, had begun to permeate the air.

"I never saw the boat," the mayor said easily, his ease perhaps slightly artificial. "It belonged to a fellow named Le Glen, or Le Glérec, who was said to be an excellent seaman but hotheaded. Like all the coasters in this area, the *Pretty Emma* mainly carried early vegetables to England . . . One fine day, she apparently sailed on a longer voyage. There was no news for two months. Eventually, we heard that the *Pretty Emma* had been searched when it arrived at a small port near New York. Its crew was sent to prison, and the cargo—cocaine—was seized. The boat, too, of course . . . That was at the time when most freighters, especially those that carried salt to Newfoundland, were involved in smuggling liquor."

"Thank you . . . Stay where you are, Léon. Answer me from there . . . And answer the questions I ask you exactly, and *nothing more*! You hear me? . . . First, where did they arrest you just now?"

The vagrant, wiping at the blood on his chin, said in a hoarse voice, "At Rosporden . . . in a railway station, where we were waiting till dark to jump onto a train."

"How much money did you have?"

It was the lieutenant who answered: "Eleven francs and a little change."

Maigret looked at Emma, whose cheeks were wet with tears, then at the brute, now silent and withdrawn. He sensed that the doctor, though quiet, was intensely agitated, and he signed to one of the policemen to station him-self near Michoux, ready for any eventuality.

The sergeant was still writing. His pen scratched on the paper with a metallic sound.

"Tell us, exactly, the circumstances of this cocaine cargo, Le Glérec."

The man raised his eyes. His gaze locked on to the doc-tor and grew hard. His mouth bitter, his heavy fists clenched, he muttered, "The bank had lent me money to get my boat built . . ."

"I know that. Go on."

"It was a bad year. The franc was rising. England was buying less produce. I was worried about paying the inter-est . . . I wanted to get most of the loan paid off before I married Emma . . . Then this newspaperman looked me up. I knew him because he hung around the port a lot . . ."

Astonishing everyone, Ernest Michoux dropped his hands from his face. It was pale, but infinitely calmer than anyone expected. He drew a notebook and a pencil from his pocket and wrote a few words.

"Did Jean Servières offer you a cocaine shipment?"

"Not right away. He only talked about doing some business. He told me to meet him in a café in Brest. He was waiting there with two other men—"

"Dr. Michoux and Monsieur Le Pommeret?"

"That's right."

Michoux jotted down some more notes, his expression disdainful. At one point he even gave a sardonic smile.

"Which of the three actually gave you the job?"

The doctor waited, his pencil poised.

"None of them . . . That is, they just talked about the big money I could make for a month or two's work . . . . An American turned up an hour later. I never heard his name, and I saw him only twice. He obviously knew the sea, because he asked me the specifications of my boat, the number of men I'd need on board, and how much time it would take to install an auxiliary engine . . . I figured what they had in mind was bootlegging liquor. Everyone was doing some of that, even officers on the liners . . . The next week, workmen came to install a semi-diesel engine on the *Pretty Emma* . . ."

He spoke slowly, his gaze fixed. But the slow, spasmodic movements of his huge fingers were more eloquent than his face, and it was affecting to watch them.

"They gave me an English chart that showed Atlantic wind patterns and routes for sailing vessels, because I'd never made the crossing . . . Being cautious, I took only two men with me, and I never told anyone about it but Emma. She was on the jetty the night we left . . . The three Frenchmen were there too, standing next to a car with its lights out . . . We'd taken on the cargo that afternoon. And at that moment, as we set out, I got scared . . . Not so much about the contraband. But I never had much schooling. As long as I can use the compass and the plumb line, I'm all right; I can do as well as anyone. But out there on the open ocean . . . An old sea captain had tried to teach me how to use the sextant to take bearings. And I bought logarithm tables and all that. But I was sure to get tangled up in the calculations . . . Still, if I made it, the boat would be paid for and I'd have about twenty thousand francs left . . . There was a terrible wind that night. We lost sight of the car and the three men. Then Emma, her dark shape at the end of the jetty . . . Two months at sea . . ."

Michoux was still taking notes, but he avoided looking at the man speaking.

"I had landing instructions. Finally—God knows how—we got to the little port they'd told us about . . . But before we even threw out the anchors, we were surrounded—three police launches with machine guns and men carrying rifles. They jumped on deck, held us at gunpoint, and shouted things in English. They hit us with the rifle butts till we put our hands up . . .

"All we saw was the gunfire—it happened so fast. . . . Somehow my boat was tied up to the pier, and we got shoved into a van. An hour later, we were each locked up in a separate cell, at Sing Sing . . .

"We were ill. Nobody spoke any French. The other prisoners made jokes and yelled insults at us . . .

"Things go fast over there. The next day, we went before some kind of tribunal, and the lawyer who was supposed to be defending us never said a word to us! . . .

"Afterward, he told me I was sentenced to two years of hard labor and a 100,000-dollar fine, that my boat was confiscated . . . and a lot I didn't understand. A hundred thousand dollars! I swore I didn't have any money. That meant I don't know how many extra years in prison . . .

"I stayed at Sing Sing. My men must have been put in

another prison, because I never saw them again . . . They shaved my head . . . They put me in a road gang, smashing rocks . . . There was a chaplain who tried to give me Bible lessons . . .

"You can't imagine what it was like. There were rich prisoners who went off into town almost every night . . . and they used the rest of us as their servants! . . .

"It doesn't matter. After a whole year of that, one day I ran into the American from Brest. He was visiting another prisoner. I recognized him, and called to him. It took him a while to remember. Then he burst out laughing and had me brought to the visiting room.

"He was very cordial . . . treated me like an old friend. He told me he'd been a Prohibition agent. He worked abroad mostly, in England, in France, in Germany; he'd send the American police information on shipments leaving from there.

"But at the same time, he occasionally did some trafficking for himself. That was the case with that cocaine shipment, which was supposed to bring in millions, because there were ten tons aboard at who knows what price per ounce . . . So he'd got together with some Frenchmen, who were to supply the boat and part of the investment— that was my three men—and naturally they would split the profits among the four of them . . .

"But listen! The best part is coming . . . The very day we were loading at Quimper, the American got word from back home: there was a new Prohibition chief, and surveillance was going to be stepped up. Buyers in the United

States were holding off, and for that reason the merchandise might not find a taker . . .

"At the same time, a new order said anyone who informed on prohibited cargo would get a bounty, as much as a third of its value . . .

"There I was in prison hearing this! . . . He told me that, at the moment I was casting off—worried sick about whether we would even reach the other side of the Atlantic alive—he was in the car, and my three men were arguing with him, there on the quay.

"Should they gamble on getting through, for the whole stake? . . . I know now that it was the doctor who held out for informing on me. At least that way they'd be sure of getting a third of the money, with no complications.

"Not counting that the American had made a deal with a colleague to skim off part of the impounded cocaine. An unbelievable racket, I know! . . .

"The *Pretty Emma* glided out on the dark water of the harbor . . . I took one last look at my fiancée, telling myself I'd be back to marry her in a few months . . .

"And they knew—those men watching us leave—they knew we'd be picked up when we got there! They'd even figured that we'd put up a fight, that we'd probably be killed in the struggle. It was happening every day in American waters at the time . . .

"They knew that my boat would be confiscated, that it was not entirely paid for, and that I had nothing else in the world. They knew my one dream was to marry Emma. And they watched us go!

"That's what the American told me at Sing Sing, where I'd turned into an animal, among those other animals . . . He proved it to me. He laughed and slapped his thigh, and said, 'Some bastards, those friends of yours!'"

Suddenly, there was absolute silence. And in that silence could be heard the startling sound of Michoux's pencil sliding over a fresh page.

Maigret looked at the initials *S S* tattooed on the giant's hand, and understood: *Sing Sing.*

"I probably had ten years more to go . . . In that country, you never know. The slightest infraction of the rules, and the sentence gets longer, and meanwhile they go on hitting you with their clubs . . . I got hundreds of those beatings—from the other prisoners, too . . . Then my American took steps to help me. I think he was disgusted by the behavior of those men he kept calling my 'friends' . . . The only company I had was a dog. I raised him onboard, and he'd saved me from drowning once. In spite of all their rules over there, they let him stay in the prison—they have different ideas from us about that kind of thing . . . Oh, it was hell! They'll play music for you on Sundays, and then beat you to a pulp afterward . . . Finally, I didn't even know if I was still a man. I broke down sobbing a hundred times, a thousand times . . .

"And then, one morning, they suddenly opened the door, rammed a rifle butt into my back to send me off into the civilized world, and I passed out on the pavement like an idiot . . . I didn't know how to live anymore; I had nothing left . . .

"No! I did have one thing left!"

His wounded lip still bled, but he forgot to wipe it. Madame Michoux was hiding her face in her lace handkerchief, with its sickening scent. And Maigret smoked placidly, never taking his eyes off the doctor, who went on writing.

"One thing—the determination to put them through the same hell, those men who had brought the whole catastrophe down on me. Not to kill them—no! Dying is nothing. At Sing Sing, I tried it a dozen times, but I couldn't do it. I'd stop eating, and they'd force-feed me . . . No, no! I wanted to make them live in prison! I wanted it to be an American jail, but that's not possible . . .

"I dragged around Brooklyn, doing any kind of job, to pay my way home . . . I even bought passage for my dog . . .

"I'd had no news of Emma . . . I didn't set foot in Quimper; people might have recognized me, even if I am a wreck.

"Here, I heard that she was a waitress, and Michoux's mistress now and then . . . Other people too, maybe? A waitress, after all . . .

"It wouldn't be easy to send those three bastards to prison, but I was determined! That was the only thing I still wanted . . . I lived with my dog on an abandoned boat, and later in the old watchtower at Cabélou Point . . .

"I began to let Michoux see me around—just see me. See my hideous face, my brute's body! You understand? I wanted to scare him. I wanted to stir up such fear in him that he'd be driven to shoot at me. I might wind up dead, but he'd go to prison. He'd get it all; he'd be kicked and beaten, with clubs and gun butts! And the terrible people in there with you—so strong they can make you do anything they want . . . I prowled around Michoux's house. I put myself in his path. Three days. Four days. He finally recognized me. Then he went out less . . . But still, life here hadn't changed in all that time. They still had their daily aperitif together, the three of them; people tipped hats to them in the streets . . . And I was stealing food from stalls! . . . I wanted things to happen fast."

A curt voice spoke: "I beg your pardon, superintendent. This hearing, without an examining magistrate present—I don't suppose it has any legal standing?"

It was Michoux—Michoux, white as a sheet, his features drawn, nostrils pinched, lips drained of color. But Michoux was speaking with a curtness that was almost threatening.

A glance from Maigret sent another policeman to take up a position between the doctor and the vagrant. Just in time! Drawn by that voice, Léon Le Glérec rose slowly, his fists clenched and as heavy as clubs.

"Down! Sit down, Léon!"

And the creature obeyed, breathing hoarsely as the superintendent shook out his pipe and said, "Now it's my turn to talk."

11

FEAR

His quiet voice and his rapid, even delivery were a sharp contrast to the impassioned speech of the sailor, who watched him suspiciously.

"First, a word about Emma, gentlemen: She learns that her fiancé has been arrested; she hears nothing more from him . . . One day, for some unimportant reason, she loses her job and becomes a waitress at the Admiral Hotel. She's a poor girl, with no family. Men flirt with her, the way rich customers do with servant girls. Two years, three years go by. She has no idea Michoux had a hand in Léon's fate. One night she goes to his room. Time goes by, life rolls on. Michoux has other mistresses. From time to time, he decides to sleep at the hotel. Or sometimes, when his mother is away, he has Emma come to his house . . . Dreary lovemaking, with no love to it. And Emma's life is dreary. She's no heroine. She has a shell-covered box, where she keeps a letter, a snapshot, but that's just an old dream that fades a little more each day . . .

"She doesn't know that Léon has come back.

"She doesn't recognize the yellow dog that prowls around her—it was four months old when the boat left.

"One night, Michoux dictates a letter to her, without saying who it's for. It's about an appointment with someone in an empty house at eleven o'clock at night.

"She writes it down, signing it 'E'—for Ernest, she thinks. A waitress! You understand? . . . Léon Le Glérec was right: Michoux is frightened; he's afraid for his life . . . He wants to do away with the enemy who's haunting him.

"But he's a coward. He couldn't help telling me that himself. He sends his victim the letter by tying it around the dog's neck. He figures he'll hide behind the door in the empty house the next night.

"Will Léon be suspicious? Well, there's a chance the sailor might want to meet with his old fiancée again, no matter what's happened. When he knocks at the door, Michoux will just shoot through the letter box and slip away through the back alley.

"But Léon does suspect something. Maybe he was lurking around the square, watching. Maybe he was even thinking of going to the appointment. By chance, Monsieur Mostaguen comes out of the café just then, with a few drinks in him, and stops in that doorway to light his cigar. He's a little unsteady; he stumbles against the door. That's the signal, and a bullet hits him right in the belly.

"That's the first incident . . . Michoux bungled his attempt. He goes home. Goyard and Le Pommeret are terrified. They know what's going on, and they have the same interest in getting rid of the man—he's a threat to all three of them.

"Emma understands the trick she was made to play. She may have caught sight of Léon . . . or perhaps she put things together and finally identified the yellow dog.

"The next day, I arrive on the scene. I see the three men, I sense their terror. *They're expecting some trouble!* And I want to find out where they think it will come from. I want to be sure I'm not wrong.

"So I'm the one who put the poison in the aperitif bottle, in my clumsy way . . . I'm ready to step in if someone should start to drink. But there's no need! Michoux is on guard. Michoux is suspicious of everything—of the people going by, of what he drinks . . . By now he doesn't even dare leave the hotel."

Emma was frozen, the very picture of stupefaction. Michoux had lifted his head for a moment, to look squarely at Maigret. Now he was writing feverishly again.

"That was the second incident, *Monsieur le Maire.* And our trio lives on, still in fear . . . Goyard is the most excitable of the three, and probably also the least bad. This business of the poisoning throws him into a panic. He's convinced something will happen to him one day or another. He sees I'm on the trail—and he decides to run off. Without a trace—run off in such a way that no one will be able to accuse him of running away. He'll fake an attack, let people think he's been killed and that his body was thrown into the harbor.

"But before that, something leads him to take a look around Michoux's house, maybe out of curiosity, maybe to look for Léon and offer to make peace. He finds signs that the big man has been there. He knows it won't take me long to discover the same signs myself.

"Remember, he's a newspaperman! He knows very well how easy it is to stir up a mob. He knows he won't be safe anywhere as long as Léon is alive. So he thinks up a really brilliant move: he writes an article, in a disguised hand, and sends it to the *Brest Beacon*.

"The piece talks about the yellow dog, the drifter. Every sentence is calculated to spread terror in Concarneau. In those circumstances, if people spot the man with the big feet, there's a good chance he'll get a shot of lead in his chest.

"And that's nearly what happened! They started by shooting the dog; they would just as easily have shot the man. A panicky crowd is capable of anything.

"On Sunday, terror *does* take over the town. Michoux sticks to the hotel, sick with fright. But he's still determined to defend himself to the end—*by any means*.

"I leave him alone with Le Pommeret. I don't know what goes on between the two of them then. Goyard's gone. Le Pommeret, who belongs to a respectable local family, is probably tempted to turn to the police, to tell the whole story rather than go on living through this nightmare . . . After all, what's the risk for him? A fine, a little stint in prison. If that! The major crime, the only one he had any part in, had been committed abroad, in America.

"And Michoux, who sees him weakening, who has the

Mostaguen attack on his conscience, wants to save his own skin at any cost. He doesn't hesitate to poison him . . .

"Emma is there in the café. Maybe they'll suspect her instead . . .

"I'd like to talk to you a little more about fear, because that's what underlies this whole business. Michoux is afraid. Michoux is more obsessed with conquering his fear than with conquering his enemy.

"He knows Léon Le Glérec. He knows that the man won't be stopped without a struggle. He's counting on a bullet fired by the police or by some terrified townsman to take care of that problem.

"He stays put . . . I bring the wounded dog, barely alive, into the hotel. I want to see if the vagrant will come to get him, and he does. We've never seen the dog since, and that probably means he's dead."

There was a small sound in Léon's throat. "Yes."

"Did you bury him?"

"On Cabélou. There's a little cross, made of two fir branches."

"The police find Léon Le Glérec. He breaks away, because his one goal is to incite Michoux to attack him. He's said it: *He wants to see him in prison* . . . My job is to prevent any further harm, and that's why I arrest Michoux, even though I tell him that my purpose is to protect him. It's not a lie. But, by the same move, I keep Michoux from committing other crimes. He's reached the point of being capable of anything. He feels threatened from all sides.

"Nonetheless, he's still capable of doing his little act, talking to me about his poor health, blaming his panic on some mystical idea about a fortune-teller years back—a story he invented out of whole cloth.

"What he needs desperately is for the public to decide to slaughter his enemy.

"He knows that he could quite logically be suspected of everything that's happened up till then. Alone in his cell, he racks his brain. Isn't there some way of turning those suspicions around once and for all? For instance, if some new crime were to occur while he's under lock and key, that would provide him with the most wonderful alibi for everything, by implication.

"His mother comes to see him. She knows the whole story. She's got to stay clear of suspicion, of investigation. But she's got to save him! . . .

"She dines at the mayor's. She gets herself driven home after dinner and leaves her light burning for the next few hours. Meanwhile, she returns to town on foot. Is everyone asleep? Everyone except those in the Admiral café. All she has to do is wait, at some street corner, for someone to leave the café. Then aim at his leg, to be sure he doesn't chase her.

"That crime, that completely gratuitous crime, would be the worst of the charges against Michoux, if we didn't already have others. The next morning, when I get here, he's feverish. He doesn't know that Goyard is under arrest in Paris. Most important, he doesn't know that at the very moment the shot hit the customs guard, I had the vagrant under my very eyes.

"For, with the police after him, Léon had stayed right in the same neighbourhood where they'd lost him. He was anxious to finish his business, so he didn't want to get too far from Michoux.

"He goes to sleep in a room in the vacant building. From her window, Emma sees him. And she goes over to join him. She swears that she's not guilty, that she never meant to help Michoux. She throws herself down, clings to his knees . . .

"This is the first time he's seen her face to face, heard the sound of her voice again . . . She's been with another man, a few others.

"But there isn't much he hasn't been through, himself. His heart melts. He seizes her in a brutal grip, as if to crush her, but then, instead, his lips crush hers.

"He is no longer all alone, the man with nothing to live for but a single goal, a single idea. Through her tears, she speaks to him—about a chance for happiness, a life they might begin again . . .

"And they leave together, without a sou, into the night. They'll go anywhere; it doesn't matter! . . . They leave Michoux to his terrors.

"They'll try to be happy somewhere . . ."

Maigret fills his pipe, slowly, looking at each person in the room, one after the other.

"You'll excuse me, *Monsieur le Maire,* for not letting you know what I was up to. But when I arrived here, I felt sure the drama had just begun . . . To figure out its pattern, I had to let it develop, heading off further damage as best

I could . . . Le Pommeret is dead, murdered by his accomplice. But from what I know of him, I'm convinced he would have killed himself the moment he was arrested. A customs guard was shot in the leg; in a week, it won't even show. On the other hand, I can now sign a new arrest warrant for Ernest Michoux, for attempted murder and assault on the person of Monsieur Mostaguen, and for the willful poisoning of his friend Le Pommeret. Here's another warrant, against Madame Michoux, for last night's assault . . . As to Jean Goyard, called Servières, I don't believe he can be cited for anything more than obstruction of justice with that hoax he set up."

That was the only comic moment. The plump journalist heaved a sigh, an elated sigh. Then he had the nerve to babble: "In that case, I presume I can be released on bail? I'm prepared to put up fifty thousand francs."

"The public prosecutor will determine that, Monsieur Goyard."

Madame Michoux had collapsed in her chair, but her son was more resilient.

"You have nothing to add?" Maigret asked him.

"I will answer only in the presence of my attorney. Meantime, I formally protest the legality of this proceeding."

And he stretched out his neck, a thin young rooster's neck with a yellowish Adam's apple bulging from it. His nose looked more crooked than ever. He was gripping his notepad.

"And those two?" murmured the mayor as he rose.

"I have absolutely no charge against them. Léon Le

Glérec has stated that his goal was to provoke Michoux to shoot him. To that end, he did nothing but put himself in the man's path. There's no law against—"

"Except vagrancy," put in the police lieutenant.

But the superintendent shrugged in a way that made the man blush at his own suggestion.

———————

Lunchtime was long past, but there was still a crowd outside. So the mayor agreed to lend his car, with its curtains closed almost hermetically.

Emma climbed in first, then Léon Le Glérec and, last, Maigret, who sat on the rear seat with the young woman, leaving the sailor to arrange himself awkwardly on the jump seat.

They cut quickly through the crowd. A few minutes later, they were on the road to Quimperlé. Uncomfortable and averting his gaze, Léon asked Maigret, "Why did you say that?"

"What?"

"That you're the one who put the poison in the bottle?"

Emma was very pale. She didn't dare lean back against the cushions; it was doubtless the first time in her life that she had ridden in a limousine.

"Just an idea!" muttered Maigret, clamping his pipe stem in his teeth.

Then the girl cried out in distress:

"I swear to you, superintendent, I didn't know what I was doing anymore! Michoux made me write that letter.

I'd finally recognized the dog. And on Sunday morning I saw Léon lurking around . . . Then I understood. I tried to talk to him, but he walked off without looking at me, and he spat on the ground . . . I wanted to get revenge for his sake . . . I wanted . . . oh, I don't even know! I was nearly crazy. I knew they were trying to kill him . . . I still loved him . . . I spent the whole day turning over ideas in my head. At noon, before lunch, I ran over to Michoux's house to get the poison. I didn't know which one to pick . . . He showed them to me once, and said there was enough there to kill everyone in Concarneau . . .

"But I swear I would never have let you drink . . . At least, I don't think so."

She was sobbing. Léon awkwardly patted her knee to calm her.

"I can never thank you, superintendent," she said through her sobs. "What you've done is . . . is . . . I can't think of the word . . . It's so wonderful!"

Maigret looked at each of them, at him with his split lip, his cropped hair, and his face of a beast trying to become human; at her with her poor little face faded white from living in that aquarium, the Admiral café.

"What are you going to do?"

"We don't know yet . . . Leave this place. Maybe head for Le Havre . . . I managed to earn a living on the New York docks . . ."

"Did anyone give you your twelve francs back?"

Léon flushed but did not answer.

"What's the train fare to Le Havre?"

"No! Don't do that, superintendent. Because then ... we couldn't ... You see what I mean?"

They were passing a small railway station. Maigret tapped on the glass separating them from the driver. Drawing two hundred-franc notes from his pocket, he said: "Take this. I'll put it on my expense account."

He practically pushed them out of the car and closed the door while they were still looking for words to thank him.

"Back to Concarneau. Fast!"

Alone in the car, he shrugged his shoulders three times, like a man with a strong urge to make fun of himself.

———

The trial lasted a year. During that whole year, as often as five times a week, Dr. Michoux went to see the examining magistrate, carrying a morocco briefcase crammed with documents.

At each court session he argued over something else. Every item in the dossier set off new controversies, investigations, and counter-investigations.

Michoux grew steadily thinner, yellower, sicklier, but he never gave up.

"I'm sure you'll allow a man with only three months to live ..."

That was his favorite expression. He fought every inch of the way, with underhanded maneuvers, unpredictable responses. And he had found a lawyer even nastier to back him up.

Sentenced to twenty years' hard labor by the Finistère Criminal Court, he spent six months trying to appeal his case to the higher court.

But a month ago, a photograph printed in all the newspapers showed him, still skinny and yellow, with his crooked nose, a bag on his back, and a forage cap on his head, embarking from the Ile de Ré on the *Martinière*, which was carrying 180 convicts to Devil's Island.

Madame Michoux served her three-month sentence in prison and is in Paris pulling strings in political circles. She hopes to get her son's case reheard.

Léon Le Glérec fishes for herring in the North Sea, aboard the *Francette*, and his wife is expecting a baby.